Melvina

I Hope you like
This!

The Color of Power

James lee Nathan III and Sharon Downing

Melvina

The Color of Power

James lee Nathan III and Sharon Downing

Leanpub

This is a Leanpub book. Leanpub empowers authors and publishers with the Lean Publishing process. Lean Publishing is the act of publishing an in-progress ebook using lightweight tools and many iterations to get reader feedback, pivot until you have the right book and build traction once you do.

Also By James lee Nathan III

Special thanks to the Massey family which has bestowed upon me the great honor of bringing Melvina's story to life.

Contents

CONTENTS

The Color of Power

Forward

I first met Melvina in the spring of 2016, through one of her descendants, Ms. ShaRon Downing. From the moment, I hear Melvina's 'known facts' I am intrigued and moved to contribute. This begins a journey into the incredible life of Melvina Massey.

So, as I read the various accounts of Melvina's life gathered by the family researchers, I wanted to emulate their efforts and strategy. For the last four years, Brandon Massey and ShaRon Downing dismissed the kitchen table talk, the gossip, and dug deeper into the 'known facts'. When I join the team, I add another layer of analysis to the mix.

Now, to remove the myths masquerading as truth I had to first review each fact, associated story, ancillary commentary (newspaper articles) without my 2016 'filter', which clouds my judgment. Once the filter is vanquished, I then ask why? Yet, the lack of documents and corroborative elements was discouraging and made the effort difficult.

However, another task ahead of me was to convince the Massey family that a historical fiction of Melvina's life could tell her story to the masses better than a work of non-fiction (with very little documentation). This genre (historical fiction) requires the scenes be authentic and right and consistent with the times. Any addition of real life characters and events adds a layer of depth to the story. This invites the readers to use their own mind in visualizing the scene at hand. I wrestled with adding true charismatic figures of the old west in this story.

"I have no problem with fiction, but I don't want my 3xgreat grandma in shootouts with aliens," Brandon Massey.

The real problem with writing historical fiction of real African Americans in the 19th century is the lack of corroborative documentation. Journalists and writers rarely document the exploits of larger than life nonwhites, any more than average ones. In fact, you are more likely to read of a Negro behaving 'badly' than one exceeding expectations. One hundred years later and things are the same I suppose.

A contemporary of Melvina's is the legendary Lawman Bass Reeves. A Deputy US Marshal in the volatile Indian Territory, who made over 3,000 arrests. But, to the public, he is a question mark. The dime novels that chronicle the exploits of virtuous Negro Marshals or captivating news articles in the west and east do not exist, and so these events did not occur. However, historians of the old west and court documents name the man said to be the archetype of the western Lawman.

Now juxtaposed to Bass is Melvina, the infamous Negro woman, who ran brothels and bootlegged alcohol in the dry state of North Dakota for twenty years, with more coverage than the great Bass Reeves. There is that Negro behaving 'badly' generalization in the media again. Newspaper accounts of the notorious Madam Massey are sparse, so imagine what there was for Bass, none.

Why use 'Madame' instead of 'Madam'?

Using 'Madame' is on purpose. Once again, the times dictate syntax. Madame is a polite way to address an older French woman of status. Distant relations to Melvina call her 'Madam' as she is a brothel owner. Her more personal relationships refer to her as 'Madame', to show both her marital status (she marries at the height of her power and wealth) and her refined lineage.

Melvina is not French; however, her complexion and mannerisms correspond with those expensive delicacies in the French Quarter of New Orleans, 'Storyville'. A place where mulatto Creole women are the sexual fetish of the region, and another device she uses to hide her identity. Madame (in this context) equals experience and mystery.

So why use the two different words? It is perception. Melvina (the character in this novella) throughout her life manipulates how people see her. She cultivates 'Madame Massey' to embody the exotic, seductive, elite, and foreign sexual dalliance. Melvina is a brothel owner, but she demands respect in every way. Is this a delusion of hers or a clever illusion you decide. It should be stated, the papers of the day, often called her 'Madame' as much as they reported 'Madam'.

FACTS?

So let us talk facts and what my intentions are in delivering this tale to you the reader. The facts we have, Melvina is born in 1838. She gave birth to her only child Henry in 1858. It is probable (90% sure) that Melvina is involved in two scandalous trials in 1875.

She was in the Red River Valley as early as 1881. Madam Massey builds the Crystal Palace in 1891 and marries in 1893. A bootlegging conviction in 1901 sends her to Bismarck State Penitentiary. Melvina serves only seven months of a one-year sentence and dies in 1911.

After the first review of the facts, there was a definitive gap of 33 years (1858-1891). I pressed her descendants on the details of each fact and we narrowed the gap in half. Once or twice a day, we gather, and ponder specific things in her life and seek to unravel the mysteries that still surround this extraordinary woman. This is still ongoing as we discover new and interesting tidbits of information on Melvina Massey every day. Fiction fills the gaps between actual events, yet the facts set up the story. Three different aspects of Melvina's life emerge.

First, no pictures of Melvina exist. But, we know that her father and mother were both 'mulattoes' living in Virginia. This makes Melvina a mulatto, sharing similar traits as her European grandparents such as light complexion (most times), long wavy or straight hair, and blue, green, or gray eyes (they characterized her eyes as luxurious).

So, the writing task I have is to articulate the complexities of being a mulatto woman in the 19th century with its pros and cons, and how does Melvina leverage or skirt this issue throughout her life.

Why is Melvina handled one way in the press before 1901, and then opposite after the turn of the Century? A recurring theme when dealing with Melvina. This is a perplexing issue that on one hand, supports that the town of Fargo, did not know her true ethnicity. But, town historians routinely say that 'She stood out like a sore thumb', yet have a hard time rationalizing her coverage in the papers.

Coverage that only mentions her ethnicity after her conviction (in 1901). Even when confronted with census data stating her race as 'white' in 1900, and 'mulatto' in 1910, people are adamant they always knew she was black. Now 'passing' in 2016 is not much of an issue, but during the 19th century, many passed (not just blacks/mulattos) and they did so for various reasons.

Achieving a higher social and cultural status is the most prominent. Jews changed their names, Chinese posed as Mexicans, and blacks moved west and posed as white, availing them to housing, education, employment, and less harassment. If you intend to pass, one must understand the culture you aspire to and their mannerisms. Former slaves (that worked in the big house) were privy to elegant dining, interior decorations, and formal etiquette. The average white person is unfamiliar with such a lifestyle. So this gives the impression that the person passing is a member of the gentry.

The belief is she played upon people's natural bias of

race and uses that to her gain at every turn. That is until discovered. For much of her life in the Red River Valley, her race is never in question. She is a white woman of means from Virginia (is what they believe) so why ever question her ethnicity? This perception changes at the turn of the century (with her arrest). The articles on a 'Negress' 'Colored' Madam in Cass and Clay counties underscore something that even escaped the historians. No one knew Melvina's true ethnicity until her incarceration.

Articles and records before 1901 refer to her as Melvina Massey or Madam Massey. It is only after 1901 that we see a change in their characterizations of her more of a 'disdain' or 'contempt'.

Second, what life experiences shape this woman into a power broker in the Red River Valley for a generation? The gaps in her life and history show how she traveled and when. For instance, a possibility exists that a young Melvina worked in and around DC from 1860-1868. The war limits her freedom of movement. There are no jobs for women of any race in the 19th century other than a domestic, schoolteacher, nurse/comfort aid, or prostitute. The latter being the last resort. Prostitutes followed troop movements or camp in a central location, accessible by both forces.

Regional history (Virginia, Maryland, and DC) shows a few upscale brothels from 1850-1870 that used mulattoes and European immigrants. After the war (and for the better part of 'Reconstruction') only income and access to railroads limits her ability to travel.

When did she become a Madam and how does this change her? How do politics and prostitution work together? The answer is power.

Prostitution, (in upscale elite brothels) has always gone together with power broking. For thousands of years, prostitutes were espionage tools to extract information from both enemies and allies. A prostitute (Rahab) gives the Army of Israel, access to Jericho. Information is power, and many prominent executives or politicians brag of accomplishments to prostitutes. It is a show of power, which the man transmutes to the sexual agent.

She now can use this information to her best interest. But, most of these women were pawns for the Madam who acts as a surrogate for anyone wanting access or information, blackmail or extortion. A theory is that Melvina learns the tricks of the trade (if you will) and then puts her own plan into motion, years later and becomes a major power broker in the Red River Valley.

How powerful was she? You may see documentaries, and blogs that state she was a notorious Madam who ran up to five brothels at one time in Fargo. But, what you won't hear or read is that she did this for at least 15 years, and sold alcohol in these establishments in open defiance of the State's prohibition laws. Now the town states they knew she was black. How does a black woman evade prosecution for 12 years? Fargo indicts and convicts, Melvina Massey of a crime that only one other person does time for in the state's history. She is the second and last person to be sentenced before prohibition is lifted.

How was she able to operate without reprisals? She was black (which everyone knew) and powerful. Or, Melvina Massey was a mulatto (black, but no one knew) and powerful, but subject to reprisals after she is found out. I believe she had connections in high places and she knew how to manipulate the color of power.

There are rumors and myths of power because much cannot be substantiated. Even the documentaries run into similar issues. Yet I press on and dig deeper into the facts, which prove problematic. For instance, there has always been a 'story' 'myth' of her incarceration at the Bismarck State Penitentiary.

The story goes that Melvina did not stay in the quarters for female inmates. She stayed in the Wardens house-/quarters. Newspapers of the day report this as fact but we find no documents to substantiate these claims. What we can prove is that there were female prisoner accommodations at the prison before her arrival. The state builds the warden's quarters and admin building three years before Melvina arrives, and her stay is only 7 months.

Did she use what little power she had? Or, is this kindness towards a whore in her 60s who they release early for good behavior? Yes, an interesting conundrum, however, the earlier statement makes you contemplate the limits of her power.

What I can say is that I suspect her notoriety and ethnicity caught up to her. The 'polite society', in which she has made a small fortune, enforces their laws, regardless of the perpetrator. They arrest the seductive and perceptive Melvina Massey not for bootlegging, but for bootlegging, being black, and not alerting the populace of this condition.

These major themes you will see as you read the novella. The story of Melvina Massey is both complex and contradictory with only a handful of facts. We tried to 'connect' the dots as best as possible. When a space between probability and fact exists, we change the names and locations. Articles and court documents are included so the reader can draw their own conclusions.

Last, I want to thank the Massey family. Who have entrusted this author to tell her story and bring it to life. They only want a good read and I hope this novella exceeds those expectations. It is an honor and a privilege to bring a fictional accounting of her life and times to the public.

James Lee Nathan III

'I write the stories you wanna read'

Introductions

DEADWOOD SOUTH DAKOTA 1884

Spring has come early to the far west of the Dakota Territory and with it murder. U.S. Marshal Seth Bullock arrives at the Chinese section of the boomtown of 25,000 inhabitants. Here as before, he sees a similar grotesque scene. A prostitute lies butchered and no clues exist save one, the same one the psychopathic killer has left over the last two nights.

"When did Chin discover this body?" asks Marshal Bullock.

"The Asian was feeding his pigs and found her on the wall. He thought little of it; another drunken whore in Deadwood is nothing -."

"To take notice of, yes I reckon he is right in that assessment," Bullock says as he looks over the body, its placement, and the scene. "Now how do you suppose she got this way?" he says and then sees a message written in blood above the dead body. "And here he leaves his calling card. Get this body covered and then wire a telegram to, on second thought," Marshal Bullock reneges on that order and wants to head to North Dakota instead. "Saddle up we leave for Fargo in the morning," he says.

"Fargo makes no sense Marshal, and ain't you forgetting something," the deputy asks as Bullock reads the writing over the body.

"What in the hell are you trying to say?" he asks.

"You have a court of inquiry to preside over and a Christening later in the afternoon. One takes an hour, but the inquiry depends on things out of our control," the deputy says. Seth understands his duties, civil and criminal cases need reviewing. The life of a regional Marshal comes with paperwork.

"Once again you make good sense Wilbur. We will postpone our trip to Fargo, for at least a month. Begin our investigation here, settle up these outstanding issues, and then be on our way," says the Marshal.

"You didn't mention why Fargo," the deputy says and covers the dead whore.

"Because Fargo is where she is..." he points to the name scribbled in blood. "MELVINA."

FARGO NORTH DAKOTA TRAIN DEPOT 1901

The conductor walks over to Sheriff Treadwell Twitchell and points to his pocket watch. It is a bright fall morning and Sheriff Twitchell is oblivious to the conductor trying hard to gain his attention. The Sheriff is waiting for someone. But, glances over at the conductor, motioning him to calm his fears.

He removes his own timepiece to get a proper accounting of the time.

"Hmmm she has five minutes by my watch conductor, and I will allow the lady to be 'comfortably' late," he says, "Besides this train is not going anywhere until I determine that we are ready to leave." The Sheriff sees a cherry wood coach approaching, with an escort of three older men on horseback. His prisoner is on her way.

The Party arrives at the depot, the woman passenger does not move until her riders have dismounted. She sits proud and tall, adorned in a velvet red dress, a thick black lace shawl, and matching black hat. Madame Melvina Massey is prepared to turn herself over to the Fargo authorities for transportation.

"Good morning Melvina, boys." The Sheriff says as he tips his hat and nods to the bodyguards. "That's far enough boys. I appreciate your loyalty to your benefactor, but Melvina will accompany me alone this morning." They pause and await further orders.

"The good Sheriff is right. I am his prisoner and he provides my protection now," she says and Sheriff Twitchell nods in approval. Melvina steps forward and remembers the first time meeting the Sheriff many years prior. She introduced her 'men' to him inside the 'Crystal Palace'.

Each of them possesses unique qualities to aid a woman of her stature and illegal activities. George Sands stood 6'3" tall and weighed 220lbs. His hands were three times the size of an average person's, and he uses them to beat sense into those foolish enough to upset the delicate quiet of the Palace.

Standing Bear of the Lakota, she met during her first trip to Minnesota. He is elusive and deadly with knives. The last of the men, Artemis, a freeman before the war, finds a younger mulatto woman beaten by three Union Soldiers. He fears the threat of worse crimes is imminent and steps forward with guns a blazing. Artemis was in Chicago when her heart breaks, and present when she masters her trade. It is Artemis that calls out the name that this Madame took as her own. MELVINA.

These are her men, sworn to protect her, and now she kisses each on the cheek as she departs. This is a brazen move by the mulatto Madame. It causes the officer to turn his head in embarrassment. Women kissing men in public is just not done during the latter stages of the Victorian Age, a white woman kissing an Indian and a Negro is blasphemous.

But, the taboo scene only lasts seconds. Sheriff Twitchell escorts her into the train cabin and handcuffs one of her arms to the seat. This disgusts Melvina.

"Is this necessary, where is a 63yo gonna run off to on the way to Bismarck?" she says. But her companion never blinks an eye. He motions to the conductor to get moving and the train exits the depot. The ride is one hundred and eighty-eight miles until Bismarck, which allows her the opportunity to think or not.

Melvina glances out of the window and then pulls the shades instead. Bitterness for Fargo still lingers. Now something else consumes her thoughts, a recollection of sorts. Her first time arriving in Fargo, many years and promises ago.

Chapter 1

Her mind begins to flashback to her first train ride to Fargo twenty years earlier. On that trip, she meets Mrs. Anika Marlowe and her husband Torsten. She met the husband earlier in an adjourning car. He introduced himself as a bachelor and made advances. Now she sees him for what he is, a lecherous married man seeking sexual liberties not more than 40 feet from his wife and children. Melvina despises men of Torsten's ilk, but their peccadillos provide her with a lavish lifestyle, so she tolerates them.

The wife, Mrs. Anika Marlowe, is more than courteous to Melvina, whom she mistakes as another well to do white woman. This is not strange for Melvina Massey, who is often taken as white.

"So Miss Massey what brings you to Fargo?" she asks, Melvina pauses for just a moment before responding.

"I have real estate to assess and maybe purchase in Fargo," Melvina says removing a small fan from her bag.

"Oh, where is Mr. Massey to handle these affairs? I always defer property matters to my husband Torsten." Marlowe says and looks away to see if the aforementioned Torsten is in the train car.

"No, there is no Mr. Massey and I enjoy it that way. What is your business in Fargo, or do you live here?" Melvina asks with an inquisitive grin.

She studies the wife now, "*What a couple, she is from money, he is not. She wears virginal black from head to toe so a religious person championing a cause is appropriate. They have children, yet there is a lack of intimacies between them, otherwise why is he soliciting female strangers on a train, complex, delightful, and intriguing."*

Melvina's assessment is dead on except Anika Marlowe is her biggest adversary in Fargo. The husband, that is later. However, the struggle between alpha women concerns Fargo's morality, North Dakota statehood, and the power to influence both.

Melvina discovers the couple's business in Fargo and dodges her own. She finds out that Mrs. Marlowe is busy here organizing a women's meeting to close the brothels and saloons. Marlowe gives Melvina a handbill which she looks over and then thanks the woman.

"Will you be attending with us, Miss Massey?" she asks. Melvina responds with a polite "No dear I'm afraid not." Confused Mrs. Marlowe responds, "Why may I ask?"

"I have no reason to partake in any endeavor whose sole purpose is to infringe upon my business efforts." Melvina responds and grins. A tremendous cloud of contempt now hovers between the two, and Melvina will always remember this moment as the day she made her first enemy in Fargo.

Anika Marlowe's face flushes red with embarrassment and then her eyes close ever so slight as if she has her target in sight. "Well Miss Massey, very well," she says with disdain in her voice.

The two continue their conversation along with the occasional insult sprinkled across the top. Torsten arrives and his eyes beg to Melvina *'Please do not reveal me'* as if Melvina is in the practice of exposing clients. Torsten is a client she intends to use for information and maybe personal satisfaction. *'He is handsome, in a tall Viking kind of way,'* she thinks and then glances out of her window as her eyes narrow and widen at the town coming into view.

She exits the train. Three men meet her within the depot and escort her to the grand hotel. Melvina turns her head back towards the depot to witness the Marlowe clan altogether. She smiles their way with the intended recipient fully aware of her intentions.

"That is a unique woman," Torsten says and his wife is quick to respond.

"She is an uppity whore, and you are a whoremonger. Are we going to revisit your sinful ways in our new town Torsten?" her accusation stings but the truth is painful.

"Well we are in the divorce capitol of the world, I am sure we can end this arrangement if you are no longer satisfied," he says.

"Torsten Marlowe you did not marry me for my pretty eyes, bright red hair, charming wit, and ample bosom. You married me for father's money. I don't see you going anywhere soon," she says. Torsten gathers up the children and the baggage acknowledging nothing his wife has just uttered. Such is their relationship.

The Assumptions Begin

As Melvina and her men walk to the carriage, she receives a report on the town and possible prospects for 'boarding houses'. During this time, the term female boarding houses are the polite society phrase for brothel or whorehouse.

The carriage stops in front of the grand hotel and only one man escorts Madame Massey inside, the other two (a Negro and an Indian) are not welcome. Neither is Melvina, access is no issue today. Members of the board of commerce, fall into a sycophantic stupor of salutations. Why respond to a white female investor any different?

Between the years of 1850-1905, over 8 million northern Europeans (from Ireland, Scotland, Sweden, Norway, Finland, and Germany) stream into the United States and make their way west to land and opportunity. Few if any of these folk have ever seen Negroes let alone the occasional mulatto. The likelihood they know a mulatto is in their midst is small.

This includes the one in front of them named Melvina, who comes from a long line of mulattoes and quadroons. She looks white but her blood is black. Here is an example of Melvina's manipulation in play.

Chapter 2

Checking in

BISMARCK DEPOT 1901

The train pulls into the Bismarck depot where the Sheriff escorts Melvina to an awaiting carriage. Melvina is ready for this next leg of the trip. No fear or trepidations she is arrogant, courageous, and Sheriff Twitchell is disinclined to acknowledge her demeanor.

"What makes you so content Melvina, considering your circumstances," he says.

"And what might those circumstances be Sheriff? That after operating a brothel that sold alcohol for 12 years Cass County makes an arrest. Or I was arrested period?" she says mocking him. Melvina appealed her first conviction to the Supreme Court of North Dakota and was out pending their verdict.

"The latter," he says, "given what I know of you and your business pursuits. But have you ever given any thought to why you have landed in prison dear?" he asks and holds her hand. A show of compassion or measuring her fear?

"I have given it much thought and will continue to do so, as long as promises are kept, I can manage my brief stay here," she says now cupping his hand in hers and looking him deep in the eye. "But make no mistake; I will handle the treachery, my way." She assures the Sheriff.

They arrive at the penitentiary at 2pm. Sheriff Twitchell hands her over to the care of the deputy Warden since the Warden N.F. Boucher (a warden with prison reform on his mind) is busy preparing his annual report. The penitentiary's matron escorts Melvina to a holding cage where she is booked.

Something is amiss in the proceedings. The sounds of chatter fill the room and smirks from the guards greet her. Melvina had assurances of a short stay and accommodations befitting of a woman of her station. However, the early indications are that something has changed.

She changes from her fine clothes into the more dank prison garb. Melvina is thankful that the wool smock and cotton undergarments appear clean from a recent washing. She puts on the proper prison attire, and the questions begin anew.

The clerk annotates her responses and starts with a date of birth.

"1839," she answers and then says, "I am 49." The admissions clerk misses an opportunity to correct Madame Massey.

The clerk now makes some physical assessments based on what he has read in tabloids and not the woman in front of him. Color = black. He judges her height and weight and then sputters out "Stand up tall against that wall. Hmmm, you are 5'9 more or less," he says. "Husband's name and whereabouts?" he asks.

Melvina takes a moment as if she was swallowing a bitter pill before answering.

"Henry Rae is my husband, and his whereabouts are unknown, he could be in Chicago, don't know, or care."

The clerk captures every word for posterity and then motions to an officer to his left. A clerk takes a photo of her, which will become an item of great curiosity 110 years later when it vanishes and no other image of the 'Mulatto Madame' exists.

The questions continue as do the snide and condescending remarks from one guard.

"*They made a promise. Where is the Warden?*" She thinks. Her eyes search the room looking. The clerk sees her and asks if she has misplaced an item.

"My *dignity and social status apparently, but to what purpose do questions serve now?*" she ponders before responding.

"Where is the Warden I wish to speak to him," she says then remembers her new status and says "Please?"

Her question amuses the clerk who chuckles aloud.

"No Warden for you, nigger whore. Be quiet and wait. Fetch the Warden my ass," he says and on cue, the matron arrives.

The Use of a Word

"*Is this badgering and demoralization of the inmates part of their incarceration mystique? These malcontents are not capable of the tasks assigned. Anyone can see this, and I been here five minutes. But, that word is used without inhibition, tread slow Melvina*" she thinks. Melvina follows the escorts to new accommodations.

The cells for women are next to the kitchen. Three narrow spaces needing ventilation and a cleaning. "Don't turn your nose up to these accommodations' missy. They're more than adequate for any nigger," says the matron. She knows that Melvina is neither a missy nor a nigger. But, in her mind one is correct.

"Pardon me, Miss, whatever your name is," the matron turns with a menacing scowl but Melvina does not blink. "Do you think that word is magical? Does it conjure or evoke a mystical spell to make me less than who and what I am?" Melvina asks looking the woman square in the eye.

"In your cell nigger whore," she says and Melvina moves but wants to say one last thing,

"Which word disgusts you more, since you use them both with equal affection? I think they are interchangeable in your mind," she says and then obliges.

The Color of Power

It is hard to say when the town of Fargo realizes that their most celebrated Madam is a mulatto and not a white woman of means from Virginia.

At the turn of the century, news and rumors spread across Cass County and disgusts their polite society.

Others in Moorhead and St. Paul Minnesota knows of her ethnicity and assume everyone else does too. She marries Henry Rae (a mulatto man who was passing and everyone knew). To reinforce her position based on their biases Melvina never refuses courtesies and privileges afforded white women of the day.

She accepts the hand that their bias and racist views offer and plays it (and them) to perfection. Perceptions, or views of non-whites and Jews, are very harsh in the latter part of the 19th century. It infects every part of life and bureaucracy in the United States, a great example is those prudent and diligent civil servants the census investigators.

Contrary to popular belief, census investigators for over 150 years used the same method of determining a person's race/ethnicity. They relied on the visual inspection and take into account how an individual is 'perceived' in their community. The last tools used are rules based on an individual's share of 'black blood'.

So, if a racially ambiguous person is well 'received' in the town where they live, the chances are the Census record will list them as white, as opposed to Italian, Greek, or black. This explains why many individuals identified as 'white' in one census can be found as mulatto or black in later ones. Race during the 1800s, absent of definitive physical attributes (skin color, hair texture, accent), is perception and always a means to an end.

Madame Melvina is one who learns to parlay other people's perceptions from a very early age. It is something that her father, Edward Massey, a free mulatto man, teaches her one Sunday afternoon.

Chapter 3

Perceptions are everything and nothing

1844 VIRGINIA

The year is 1844, Gloucester Virginia, and she is six. The two are fishing at a favorite spot when her father sees three men approaching from a mile away. He recognizes one man by the carriage he is driving as Maynard McGivney. Ole 'McGee' owns a plantation bordering the Massey tobacco farm (his former master) and is a notorious 'slave poacher' despised by most of the planters in the region. He is the true reason for stepped up slave patrols in Gloucester and not the Nat Turner revolts a decade prior.

People of the county respect Edward for his hunting skills and he maintains a humble existence around white folk. The fear of them seizing his property and selling him to planters in the Deep South is real. So, he keeps his head bowed, and mouth shut. His opinions stay in his head. But, his wisdom he shares at every opportunity.

Edward instructs Melvina on what to do. "Listen and remember when dealing with folks that perceive you as inferior, controlling what they see is your only leverage. Remember this and they will always underestimate you," he says, and she never forgets. "Perception," he continues "has nothing to do with how we see ourselves. White owners see us as property, even as freemen, they will always seek to dominate. We are fair skinned mulattoes, this is a blessing, and a curse. The masters despise and crave us in the same breath. They are nearby, remember what I have said," he says.

The young girl looks up and bares a toothless smile;

her crystal blue eyes a glow from the sun reflecting off the pond.

Edward has her cover one-third of the fish they have caught with a tarp and hemp. The remaining lots of fish stay out in the open or in a cloth bag put into the pond out of sight.

"Papa why are we hiding the fish?" she asks and her father places his gun inside his buckboard and stands there. "Now you sit there on top of our fish and do not say a word unless spoken to" he commands, young Melvina responds as children do "Yes sir" Edward turns to the road and sees that the party is now ¾ of a mile away.

Edward bids the men good afternoon, they exchange pleasantries, and the fish come up in conversation. Edward offers ¾ of his catch to the planter who accepts.

He motions for Melvina to get off the fish she is sitting on which he gathers and puts the catch in the white carriage. "Evil men are always on these roads Masa McGee. Po farmers gots to be more careful," he says playing small for the white man and feeding into his perceptions. The planter is very pleased.

McGee's attention turns to the young girl. He inquires as to Melvina's age and if she is reading and writing yet. Edward does not take the bait, "No sir it's agin the law to teach negroes but Masa Massey say to bring her up to the big house when she turns 12, and she will learn the ways of the house," Edward says and waits.

"Nonsense, yes it's against the law to teach a slave but you are free mulattoes and quadroons, so I see no problem with education. You send her up to my place in three winters and my wife and daughters will begin her learning." He says and Edward removes his hat and thanks the man. Edward then cautions the men to be careful on the road and they leave.

He does not intend to let Melvina step foot on that

man's plantation, a place where he breeds with his slaves. The owner keeps the children near his house, so that when they come of age, he can continue to have his way. Melvina can read and write but no one other than the family needs to know.

"Child we gave him enough to satisfy his curiosity. His perception led him to underestimate our craftiness. No matter what they say, white folk trust their eyes, remember that."

For much of her life, Melvina reacts to the perceptions of her, by feeding into the natural bias inherent in people. These perceptions of her she manipulates throughout her life. Her ability to move in and out of the world of white folk is not without pain, regret, or anguish. She accepts this emotional and often brutal ride, with great class and poise. However, Melvina still wants the one thing her status cannot give her, trust.

Chapter 4

Stabbed in the Back

1901 BISMARCK PENITENTIARY

The stench in the cell forces Melvina back into the present. She stands at the cell door so she can breathe. A male guard approaches her cell and slams a club against the bars causing Melvina to step back. He has a menacing look to him. "This room is compliments of Torsten Marlowe and Henry Rae. I will return later to see if you can still take a good poking" he says with a smile.

The matron, with her bigoted rhetoric, will not tolerate this behavior.

"Martin Cromley your shift is over in an hour and I suspect your wife is expecting you. Please don't keep her waiting," she says and walks back to the kitchen.

Melvina thought to thank the matron, and then remembers something her father once mentioned in passing, 'Contemplating the motivations of white folk will get you killed.' So, she leans against a wall in the cramped space instead.

Her emotions awash in confusion Melvina summons calm over herself. " *I sit in the midst of betrayal. But, not for long. Think woman,*" she says under her breath.

"*Is this how Torsten gets revenge? I kicked him out of my bed and the Palace in the winter of 1889. Men hold grudges a long time when sex is involved. Henry, why you Henry Rae? Girl please if anyone its Henry. He only disappointed you over the years. Money, women, lies and more lies, yet I kept letting him back into my life. He was absent during the trial. Once he finishes the betrayal he sped off to spend his Judas coins,*" she thinks. So many thoughts from over the year's race through her mind, one of joy deferred, and two that speak to her current dilemma.

One centered on her ability to read most people but not her lovers. The power of manipulation commands her focus now as her first day lingers on in the suffocating cell.

Three hours pass and the matron returns to Melvina's cell. She says nothing to Melvina but places a small stool in front of her cell and walks away. A minute later, he emerges from the shadows.

"If there is a God he is laughing, what brings you so far north away from your wife's money?" she says.

"I had to come see the once high and mighty after her fall," he smiles and lights a cigar.

"Torsten I have no time for your games," she says and moves back from the bars.

"Melvina, the one thing you have plenty of is time, and if I am not satisfied before I leave you will serve much more than a year in this filth," he says. She listens.

"Out with it then,"

"In due time Madam Massey. I want to gloat then I share," he says and then pauses for effect. "I bet you are wondering how you ever got here. Who conspired to bring you to your knees in ruin," the rat now smiles. "It is I. I am the sole architect of your demise and damnation," he says.

"Forgive me but I doubt you have the brains or the capital to devise and implement such a thing. But go on, I'm all ears," she says, knowing Torsten has the power.

"No dear, you're all fears now," he says.

"How like you."

Chapter 5

A Killer among Us

SPRING 1883-84 FARGO

In the years after her arrival, Melvina splits most of her time between Moorhead Minnesota (less than 2 miles from Fargo) and the 'Hollow'. She stakes out specific areas for her 'boarding houses' and continues to scout out the competition. The hierarchy of whores in Fargo goes from whorehouse madam to working girl in a whorehouse, to saloon girl in a bar, to whores that turn tricks out of makeshift shacks, and the streetwalker.

None of Melvina's girls worked the streets and only the older or homely ones were in the shacks. Melvina had 15 to 20 whores working for her (most looked above average for the time). Nine serviced her elite customers at the Crystal Palace (which does not exist at the time of the murders); two of them were light-skinned Negroes (not mulatto), two Blackfoot halfbreeds, three Asians, and two French Canadian white women.

The rest of her staff lives in three other boarding houses and three shacks. Older and most of the ugly whores use these shacks. Big Ass Charlotte Lange and her friend from Detroit Susanne Tyler fit this description to a tee. Susanne Tyler's (known as White Susanne because of her pale skin) face once scared a customer who ran to the Sheriff to lodge a complaint.

These two working girls rent two one-room shacks in the part of the Hollow that faces the train tracks. It is the worst part of town and the most dangerous. Standing Bear and George Sands, collect money from each of the houses and the shacks once a week.

One night Melvina pulls George aside.

"George how's the girls?" she asks with a look of fright in her eyes.

"What do you mean, how are they?" he says.

"Have you checked the shacks? I have not seen the girls for a week. It is not normal George. Be a dear and check them. Oh, and get my money too please," she says and George smiles as he saunters off towards the tracks. Melvina is not worried sending just one man on this errand. No one in their right mind is stupid enough to test George Sands, even with a gun.

George arrives at the location and covers his nose and face from the smell emanating from the two apartments. He enters after shouting for them each twice, and that is when he discovers the bodies. Butchered and bludgeoned beyond recognition, he hurries out of the shack and vomits. Then once he has regained his composure, he motions to a few onlookers to get the Sheriff, and he uses a word not heard in Fargo, MURDER. The law moves in to calm the fears of the town and to clean up the vagrants near the scene.

WCTU Antics

Anika Marlowe and two other members of the Women's Christian Temperance Union (WCTU) march right into the Sheriff's office. Sheriff John Haggart entertains the women.

"Mrs. Marlowe if you please, my inquiries into the two murders are ongoing, and we have ceased activities in that part of town -." he is interrupted by the quick-witted Mrs. Marlowe.

"Well, since you mentioned it," she says. The Sheriff is confused. "Sheriff Haggart, there is something we want to propose," she says and the law officer sits fearing that he has opened himself to an even worse compromise. "Given the recent developments and your own admission of an ongoing investigation, we propose that the saloons and brothels close or at the least impose a curfew until the culprit is brought to justice," she says luring him into her web. Haggart is suspicious.

"Why do you have it in for the saloon and brothel owners?" he asks as he looks around his office for the spittoon, then realizes he is in the company of uppity Christian women. He raises his coffee mug to his face and spits in it instead.

"Why Sheriff, what in the world do you mean?" says Mrs. Marlowe feigning righteous indignation at the man's implications. "Acts 3:19 'Repent, therefore, and turn back, that your sins may be blotted out'" she replies but the Sheriff is unmoved.

"Ma'am, did you recite the lord's word in my office? Do I enter your place of worship citing the penal code? Please respect the separation of Church and State and refrain from any further religious incantations on these government grounds," he says. Haggart pauses then spat right in front of the women.

"Now then please speak to your direct intentions and why you see fit to render these establishments, which are operating within the bounds of the law mind you and their owners incommunicado?" he says and sits. Mrs. Anika Marlowe is flushed with not only surprise but anger too. She lashes back at the Sheriff with a calm aggression that signals her remarkable debating skills.

"Kind sir I can assure you and the territorial judge, that my," she catches herself "Our intentions are far from self-serving. We are committed to shielding this fair town and territory, from the ravages of alcohol. We seek to remove the pestilence from here and we are more than willing to work within the bounds that the law permits," she says and her followers nod in approval. The Sheriff is still skeptical.

"I will let you ladies in on how this small municipality pays for public services such as my deputies, trash pickup, the provisioning of telephone and telegraph services, etcetera. They are funded through the fines and taxes we collect on the so-called 'parlors of sin' you seek to eradicate without an alternate suggestion for revenue," he says and the women are dumbfounded. "Never the less, you leave me no other possible way, other than to agree to your requests. A curfew on establishments in the Hollow will be at dusk until further notice. Good day," he says and pulls out more chew out of his boot.

The women leave content from his office and Mrs. Marlowe chalks up another small victory. Most citizens of Fargo view the sin in the bowels of the 'Hollow' as 'necessary evils'. These establishments offer needed revenue to the growing town. There are only 12 saloons and 8 known bordellos (Melvina ran three) in Fargo at the time of the murders.

The Mayor imposes a curfew on the saloons at dusk and the merchants of sin in the 'Hollow' are not happy. Every brothel is closed. But, after one month of low sin taxes, the town leaders withdraw from the closures altogether.

Seducing a Fool

Melvina senses a change in the business climate and tries to fend off the WCTU as best she can. A week after the curfew is lifted She offers a 'poke and a pint' night three times a week to lure customers back into her establishments. For a week or two, the business strategy works, and then the WCTU switch tactics. WCTU members stand in front of the brothels and shame the men that enter and leave. This creates a deep hate among the other madams and Melvina contemplates other measures.

The WCTU is growing in power and political connections in the territory. Two things Melvina is lacking in Fargo and her window of opportunity is closing fast. The WCTU and their supporters are sure that North Dakota will come into the union as a dry state, and one needs booze in a brothel. Melvina is reading the writing on the wall.

She sets out to subvert the efforts of the WCTU and win favor with more of the town's elite and Torsten Marlowe is easy pickings. She sends word for him at his favorite saloon and he comes. The trap is set.

Torsten arrives at Melvina's brothel on the same lot of land that the Crystal Palace will stand in six more years. Artemis and Standing Bear, who stand watch outside the door, escort him to her room. Her bed is lavish and ornate with silks; a decorative rug covers the floor. Window dressings are a mix of dark and light hues that match the fabric of her loveseat and chairs.

Torsten is charmed as Melvina receives him wearing only a silk robe and a glass of bourbon. Within minutes, Torsten is upon her, forcing the Madame to calm him.

"Slow yourself young steed, we have yet to discuss the terms of this engagement," she kisses him and nibbles his bottom lip in a tender fashion. This sends him into a sex-charged frenzy, which she re-directs. "So tell me your requirements sir," she insists. Torsten pulls away from her perfumed bosom long enough to spill his guts.

"I have longed for you the moment our eyes met on the train," he says and she interjects.

"Yet you wait 18 months before showing me any affection or trying to poke me? This does not sound like lust Torsten. It sounds like you were being a good boy," she teases him and unbuttons his britches. "Oh my, you need draining. How does a man get this way with a wife at his beck and call?" she says continuing to massage his groin making his eyes roll back in ecstasy.

She reaches up and slaps him across the face. "Wake up dear heart I need you conscious so you know what I want," the man nods and mumbles his acceptance. She resumes stroking him and delivering a message for his ears alone. "My hands are soft, do you enjoy my touch, how my hands caress your hungry areas? Good, I will touch you this way and much more each time you come with news of your wife's WCTU coven of Witches," she says and notices a change in him once the wife is mentioned, so she moves in more. "Ahh you dislike the notion of her, do you? But you enjoy my mouth, and my touch," she says and arousal returns to him. "Information is important. So, once a week, when you have news, come and I will give you a wet and delicate treat," her hand strokes the man into pure submission, and once he agrees to her terms, she relinquishes her grip.

She leans back on her bed, exposing herself to him but the months of sexual inactivity prove to be too much to overcome. "Aww you cannot have this treat because he has exploded. Tsk tsk, it will be here the next time when you bring me news," she kisses him and sucks his bottom lip before twirling away from his grasps. She pushes a button and two men enter to escort the disheveled Mr. Marlowe from the premises. He welcomes the opportunity to be her lackey, but, he has plans of his own.

A Bad Husband is no Husband

Over the following weeks, the tryst between Torsten and Melvina becomes both bold and passionate inviting suspicions from a formidable wife. Anika Marlowe puts her personal issues aside in favor of her political ambitions. She keeps a watchful eye on Torsten's activities though just so he knows that she knows.

One day he tests her knowledge by coming home earlier than usual and sees his wife holding court with members of the WCTU. Torsten notices a new figure in amongst the women. A young Baptist preacher, who is beguiling to the women, commands the floor.

Torsten watches and listens. His intention is to gather as much information as possible for Melvina. Yet he senses something else at play taking shape in his parlor. He cannot put his finger on it but he knows this meeting is the catalyst of something much bigger. So, he listens and learns.

"Ladies let us all be in agreement that the current state of affairs that promulgate the debauchery within this territory cannot and will not continue," he says. His name is Pastor Till Forrester. The women rise in solidarity and admiration. Anika embraces the pastor. This scene is unsettling to Torsten.

'My ice-hearted wife has developed an affection for the pastor, I wonder is it mutual?' he ponders. Then an unfamiliar feeling takes hold of him as he watches his wife and the pastor. Jealousy and hate fill his veins as he bears witness to a burgeoning respect and love between the two of them.

One may assume Torsten delighted with the attraction between the two, but that is not his nature. The nature of this narcissistic control freak is to keep his control. So now, he contemplates how to extract his wife from the other sycophants without causing a scene.

"Play the role of 'disinterested husband' Torsten," he ponders. An idea emerges, and he then announces his presence in an abrupt and awkward manner. He stumbles

into the room knocking over a small table.

"Oh dear I am so sorry for the intrusion ladies, and pastor my sincerest apologies. A congregation in my parlor is a surprise. Now, if it pleases those gathered a word with my wife if you don't mind," he says and Anika excuses herself. The two scurry into an adjacent hallway and the scolding begins.

"What in tarnation is wrong with you Torsten Marlowe, did I not tell you the committee meeting is not over until 930," she screams but no louder than a whisper. Torsten begs forgiveness and asks how much longer. "I don't know we were trying to wrap things up and adjourn. The Streets are not safe with that madman running free," she says.

"Yes I suppose but you women of virtue need not worry unless members of your group have a penchant for random and dangerous sex," he says just to get a rise out of her. Anika does not bite.

"You would say such a thing. Why are you home early tonight, your whore have other clients?" this bitter contentious relationship is frayed in many places, chief among them are love and respect.

"Anika if my external affairs worry you then why continue to let me back in your bed?" he says and looks back into the parlor but the women are too preoccupied with the pastor. He seizes the moment, pulls Anika to the side away from their view, and kisses her with passion. She fights off his unwanted alcohol induced lust, but to no avail, she submits. "There, you claim to be dispassionate but your mouth says different," he says.

"You disgust me, wait outside until we are through here," she says regaining her composure. "Oh and Torsten plan on sleeping outside with your cigars and contemptuous heart," she says before entering the parlor.

Torsten smiles and waits outside lighting a cigar. He

contemplates how to destroy two powerful women in his life. One he has set in motion the remaining woman will take time. By statehood, he intends to have their entire wealth.

A Meeting in the Alley

Torsten lights up his cigar and thinks back on an interesting meeting he had with a trifling man 18 months prior. It happnes after Melvina mocks both men. Well, she mocks Torsten; the other man she beats for being too rough with her whores.

The two meet by happenstance at a saloon in Fargo. Torsten is a master of manipulation, which contradicts his current relationship with Melvina. Then again, sex is the one thing he relinquishes control over unless it involves his wife.

The battered man who can't talk given his broken jaw sparks up a conversation. So he listens and Torsten talks.

"No need to further mangle the English language. That jaw will require setting before it gets worse. I know an accomplished doctor just over the bridge in Moorhead who will tend to you proper," he says and waves off the man's questions. "It's no bother; my wife has plenty of money. The money she spends on righteous causes instead of a bigger home and finer things. So paying the doctor is not a problem," he says and now plants a seed.

Torsten orders up a bottle of whiskey and the bartender pours two shots. Torsten needs the alcohol to kick his mind into gear and his drinking buddy requires something to numb the pain.

"That top whore Melvina has balls I swear," he says, and the stranger nods in agreement and mumbles something else that Torsten ignores. "She needs to be taught a lesson; in fact, all whores need to be reminded of their proper station in life. Cum buckets is all they are," he says and motions for another shot.

Torsten now makes sure not to talk too loud or bold. Innocent bystanders will use such talk for a poke. So he continues on baiting the drifter with talk of uppity whores and spiteful retribution. Over the next two hours, Torsten rams home the constant reminder to the drifter that his problems in life revolve around whores and their master Melvina.

He stuffs 50 dollars in the man's pocket and sends him off to Moorhead to the doctor and later, suggests a trip to Deadwood. "There," he says, "the whores know their place, and if they get out of line, no one cares if you straighten 'em out," these words stick in the man's head.

"*Little minds are fragile, so they only need to focus on one task at a time,*" Torsten ponders as the cigar smoke engulfs his head.

The WCTU committee members adjourn and leave the house. Torsten tips his hat to the women and pastor. "Yes sir, I will keep a close eye on your activities," he mumbles under his breath. He turns and sees Anika in the doorway, and wonders if she suspects his plans for her tonight. Each time he forces himself on her, a pregnancy results. Four times and four children age 10, 7, 5, and 3. She turns to him and slams the door behind her. He waits two hours to begin her nightmare.

Chapter 6

You can have Him

1884 FARGO

The contentious nature of the WCTU led by Mrs. Marlowe becomes unbearable for Melvina's criminal enterprises. There are face-to-face confrontations near her brothels with evangelicals and whores sometimes coming to blows.

Melvina and Torsten are in their third week of their scandalous affair, which most in the town know but never say a word. One day Melvina inflames the entire issue with a provocative and arrogant display.

She walks out of the brothel wearing only silk lavender lingerie and pearls. A carriage awaits, and she takes the reins. The Madame is determined to embarrass and shame Anika (the chief of her woes) by returning Torsten's hat to his residence.Throughout the town, people look in astonishment at her brutal, disregard for cultural norms. What upsets the 'moral code' most is not her dress but that a woman dare drive a carriage by herself.

A crowd gathers as Melvina walks across the porch and to the front door. She reaches out and raps on the door with three hard knocks. Anika answers and is aghast. Looking past her unwelcomed guest, she sees a crowd and realizes that civility will not rule this day.

"Melvina the whore, I thought your kind only came out at night," she says and Melvina responds in kind.

"Oh sugar, when it comes to the light, I'm better than the truth," she says. "Now can you and your spinsters refrain from your daily demonstrations at my houses," she says, and the stunned Mrs. Marlowe responds with the ubiquitous...

"In all of my days -," to which Melvina continues her tongue-lashing.

"Now I said to myself 'Melvina why are so many of these uppity religious sycophants, in proximity to a sin parlor in the first place?' and then it hits me, they're here because they want a poke and a pint too," she says drawing not only Anika's ire but her fury too.

"Well I never," she shouts back in Melvina's face.

"Oh, I bet you have," Melvina says folding her arms across her chest. "And if you haven't I suggest you cease your activities and maybe you can get some. Oh, he left this last night," she hands Torsten's Bowler hat to Anika. "I will bring his underwear when I have had them cleaned, or do you want to do that?" she did not wait for an answer; the look from Mrs. Marlowe says enough "YOU HEFFA." Not a good thing for Melvina and the Saloon owners, this little skirmish only emboldens the WCTU who one day later, set up day-long picket lines in front of every bar and brothel. The women sing hymns and pass handbills. They are standing between men and their sinful ways. Business suffers.

But the sun always shines for Melvina, a famous sheriff from Deadwood (Seth Bullock now a US Marshal) visits Fargo two months after the murders, seeking information on the Fargo homicides. His hope is to connect them with that the three murdered whores in his town too. Melvina is key in his investigation since the dead women (Lange and Tyler) once worked for her.

Liars and Alliances

Sheriff Haggart arrives at his office at 730am each morning without fail. Today he opens the door to find a deputy of his entertaining three men. he only recognizes Seth Bullock.

"Well if this ain't a surprise and early morning surprises are never good. So if you gentlemen don't

mind, we can suspend the formalities," he says tipping his hat to Seth. "I know the good Marshal, and appreciate if he begins with the details of this here visit, whilst I get me a cup of coffee and chew," he says.

Bullock wastes no time.

"Sheriff, we both have a similar problem of late," he begins.

"Tell it," responds Sheriff Haggart "Winslow why in the hell is there no clean coffee cups? Go on Marshal I apologize," he then finds a clean cup and pours coffee.

"Dead whores Sheriff, dead whores," Bullock says and helps himself to the cup of coffee the Sheriff just poured. "Dead whores in Fargo may be the key to this," he says. Haggart is not convinced.

"So can I hear what you're postulating or is that a surprise too?" says Haggart as he breaks off a chew. Bullock removes

his hat and takes a seat. There is a long uncomfortable pause before he recommences with revealing his thoughts.

"I believe the killer came from here, wronged emerges in Deadwood to take out revenge," he says and now has Haggart's attention. "Now the only thing I have to tie the two separate incidents together is what's at the crime scene in Deadwood," he pauses.

"I dont like suspense," he says. "Terrible for the bladder," says Haggart.

"The killer wrote a name above the victims in their blood. He wrote 'MELVINA'," he says and Sheriff Haggart spits out his chew across his desk and coughs hard. A deputy rushes to his aid. Among the chaos, Bullock pours himself another cup.

"Melvina Massey, the killer wrote her name?" screams Haggart now standing but still beet red in the face.

"No, the killer wrote Melvina, and now you have confirmed that there is a Melvina Massey living here in Fargo. Can you please take me to her?" Bullock asks wanting to keep the town's Sheriff involved in every piece of the ongoing investigation.

"I sure can. The fetching Melvina Massey is one of our Madams. She runs three brothels in the Hollow. You think she may have slighted someone and they're going around killing whores to prove a point?" asks Haggart.

"Either that or they're trying to intimidate. However, intimidation works best when the person you are trying to intimidate knows and feels the fruits of the intimidation. There is no doubt in my mind that Miss Massey has no clue what happened to those 'soiled doves' in Deadwood," he says and stands, time to move out.

"If it was your intention to lead me to a logical conclusion, well you lost me," Haggart says and follows Bullock out of the office and onto the sidewalk.

"Our killer was practicing and now is ready for more. His next move will be Moorhead, considering what I know of Miss Massey," Bullock is shrewd and methodical. He has tracked the killer back to Fargo, however; he needs the Madam to fill in the gaps of his story.

"So Madam Massey is the key, which means she has the leverage in this conversation," Haggart says and smiles.

"Why is that a concern, we are the damn law," Bullock says and then lights a cigar.

"Mmm hmm you have neither met nor ever dealt with Madame Massey my friend. Everything matters. Oh and make sure you wipe your damn feet when you walk into her place," he says and Bullock rolls his eyes in response.

"I thought we were going to a brothel," he says and

Sheriff Haggart spits out a wad of chew.

"You best wipe your feet is all," he says.

Applying Leverage

The two men arrive at Melvina's main boarding house and enter under the watchful eye of George Sands. Bullock wipes his feet.

"Big George we are not here for the regular services, we need to talk to your boss lady. Could you fetch her please?" Haggart says and makes himself comfortable.

Bullock walks through the foyer and into the parlor admiring the small but quaint accommodations. Within two minutes, she arrives, but he could smell her scent long before a physical presence enters the room. Her perfume hovers atop the cigar smoke and into his nostrils.

When he turns, an overwhelming wave known as her beauty flows across him. Haggart stands and fumbles with the introductions but apologizes for the intrusion. Bullock turns his head at this, annoyed given they are law enforcement and she is, well a prostitute. He manages a smile and tells a story.

"Miss Massey I am investigating murders in Deadwood and I believe you may be connected with... " He says and notices

no change in the demeanor of his host. "The investigation has led me to you and Fargo Madam Massey."

"This intrigues me, Deadwood did you say?" she does not wait for a verbal acknowledgment from Bullock, instead, she steers the discussion her way. "I hear the Gem is quite an establishment, and I fancy Mr. Swearengen is quite a character too," she says as she receives a cup of tea from Artemis. The rest of the party receives none.

"Miss Massey I –."

"Melvina please, call me Melvina," she insists of Marshal Bullock.

"Melvina we are not here to discuss the Gem or that ass Swearengen. I am here to discuss and inquire -."

"No Mr. Bullock you are here to tell me how I can help you, and I have just provided you with how you can reward me for my help," she says and sips her tea. Bullock is flummoxed.

"Wait so if I'm a tool I'd appreciate knowing to what purpose and for how long?" he says.

"Mr. Bullock I will provide you with all the information you desire as long as you introduce me to Mr. Swearengen. How's that my hammer?" she says and sips her tea.

"You do not understand what I came here for, nor what I could want, but you will help me still the same and all I have to do is introduce you to that rat bastard Al?" he questions.

"It's simple deduction. You are the Sheriff...no correction Marshal in Deadwood so I assume that something that occurred there has led you here. What evidence or statement are you pursuing that calls out 'Melvina' to you all the way down in Deadwood dear man?" Melvina now stands and walks over to a window. For no particular, reason other than to create a sense of theatrics, and to ensure that his eyes remain on her.

"The killer wrote the name Melvina, and the victims were whores," he says.

"So, do we have a deal Marshal?" she says, which once again catches the Marshal off guard.

"Yes I will introduce you to that asshole..." he says. "and escort you to Deadwood. Now please can you assist us or not?" Bullock loses his composure but Melvina moves across the room to stifle his thoughts.

"Shhh shhhh noble man," she says as her lips almost touch his. "We have our deal and now I will fulfill my part of the agreement," she says and removes herself from his expected grasp. "Mr. Bullock, have you met my men?" Melvina waves her hand as if it held a magic wand. Marshal Bullock looks and sees three new members in the room. He acknowledges their presence but cannot remember when they joined.

"No," he says and stands.

"The man on your right is Artemis. There is no one faster on the draw, or as deadly accurate with either a Colt or a Smith & Wesson revolver in either hand," she says but Bullock does not seem impressed. Then as if on cue, Artemis pulls his waistcoat back to reveal a double holster. This movement elicits a cautionary reaction from both officers, who reach for their holstered weapons only to realize that Artemis has already drawn and cocked his guns.

"I have seen many that were quick on the draw but not very accurate," he says.

"Gunslingers have a short lifespan. Artemis is 37. To his left is Standing Bear of the Lakota. He can track anyone or anything and shred it to pieces with his knives if need be. Last, is George Sands. One look at George and you get the picture," she smiles at both officers and then sits so Artemis can refresh her tea.

"Gentlemen it is a pleasure, now Melvina can you please tell me what the fuck you know of these murders," he says and then looks at George who takes a step towards him, but stops when Melvina speaks.

"A year ago a very brutish man came into one of my establishments and roughed up a girl. I dislike when that happens, and my men dislike when that happens. He leaves, without further incident, only to return to another one of my houses to repeat the same fiendish act. His name is Charlie Harrell," she sips her tea and then resumes. "Mr. Sands removes Charlie this time and set him on his way. That is after George broke an arm and his jaw. He screamed my name the entire time."

"Where were you?" Bullock asks as he looks at Haggart. "No let me guess, Haggart you leave them be as long as it doesn't result in a murder I suppose,"

"Mmm hmmm Seth, I see no need in filling up my jail with drunken whoremongers who get out of line. If the Madams can keep them under control, so be it. I've only come to the Hollow to sort out one matter and it had to do with how ugly a whore was," he says.

The two continue comparing law enforcement best practices for areas of illegal activities and Melvina grows impatient with the discourse.

"If I may continue..." the men apologize for the distraction. "Charlie headed south and Standing Bear tracks him to Deadwood. That is all, " she says.

"So you knew this man had returned to Fargo?" Bullock asks beating Sheriff Haggart to the punch.

"Something did not sit right with me so I had Standing Bear keep an eye out near the tracks where the vagrants, drifters, and various low life transients congregate. Within two days, he sees Charlie," she says causing both men to stand.

"So my number one suspect was here and you said nothing to law enforcement, is he still here?" Bullock screams but Melvina remains calm and collected.

"I could not assume his guilt, and besides he never stepped foot in any of my establishments so why should I care?" she says.

"Until two whores end up as dead as a priest's pecker in a whorehouse," says Haggart, Melvina raises an eyebrow and continues.

"However, the law found a vagrant dead by those tracks. Seems he fell asleep out there. So to answer your question, I suspect Charlie is still here, here as in boot hill," she puts her teacup down and looks at both men who have nothing new to add.

"Oh, my..." the Sheriff says as he remembers. "We found parts of an unknown fella by the tracks a few weeks back. Mortician had to piece him together for burial. I guess that was our man all along," Haggart suggests, and Bullock is peeved but done is done.

"I dislike how this ended dammit. But, I will leave you to any further investigations of possible crimes in Cass County. Miss Melvina a deal is a deal, I expect you to be ready in the morning -." Melvina holds up her hand to stop any further discussion.

"I am ready now sir, I have a change of wear in the bag George is holding. Anything else I need can be purchased in Deadwood," she says and smiles once again catching Bullock off guard.

Chapter 7

Let's discuss this further

1884 ON THE WAY TO DEADWOOD SOUTH DAKOTA

Keeping to his part of the bargain, Marshal Bullock escorts Melvina Massey to Deadwood. They board a train heading west and the Marshal decides on where to board the stagecoach for the rest of the trip. A coach to Deadwood takes three days to make the 300-mile trip. Bullock and his deputy arrived on horseback but agree to make the ride back in the morning with Melvina.

The train ride is uneventful; but, the stagecoach is another story. Melvina notices the 'Rules of the coach' posted in the depot.

'Rules of the coach':

'1 - Forbidden topics of discussion are stagecoach robberies and Indian uprisings;

2 - Gents guilty of unchivalrous behavior toward women passengers will be put off the stage. It is a long walk back. A word to the wise is enough;

3 - And do not snore loud while sleeping or use your fellow passenger's shoulder for a pillow. He or she may not understand and friction may result.'

These were actual rules which Melvina thought to be obvious.

The coach is comfortable and only three other passengers ride to Deadwood. Bullock ignores them and their idle chatter, however, he inquires why Melvina desires to meet Al.

"What do you know of Mr. Swearengen Melvina?" he asks.

"My business is my own Marshal Bullock," she says drawing another question and concern from the Marshal.

"Ma'am I mean not to intrude on any business you believe you have with the aforementioned pig, but I will offer advice on dealing with the devil," he says.

"Marshal, how do you suspect that a man such as him has prospered so well in Deadwood?" she asks.

"I suppose when surrounded by dirt you have to get dirty. But even in such filth, honor exists," he says with conviction.

"Marshal there is no honor in an immoral act," she says and the other two passengers turn away.

"Yet here we are on our way to meet the devil so you can take notes," his words strike a nerve, and Melvina engages him on his own terms.

"Marshal, I live in a town where folks pray on Sunday but sin Monday thru Saturday, and find great comfort within their own hypocrisy. The world is full of those who peddle temporary hope and pleasure. To survive in such a contradiction I need power, and I believe this man has tapped into such a reservoir," she says and eases back in her seat.

"What makes you believe that he will share or embolden to enlighten you of his ways and methods. Isn't that cutting against the grain so to speak," he says seeing that Melvina has taken the discussion up a notch.

"What do you understand of powerful men Marshal? They love to brag and boast of their accomplishments and conquests. Do you know why they share the essence of their success? I can tell you of a task; because I have done a task. But, that does not mean you can replicate my success," she says. And this time there can be no doubt, Melvina Massey understands how to manage power. So she searches for answers on how to gain and cultivate it.

"My God woman, I believe you know what you're heading into. Regardless of that epiphany, I will not leave your side while you engage that rat bastard, and you will stay as a guest in my home. We have meager accommodations but I think they will suit you fine."

Melvina smiles and thanks her companion and their focus turns to children and his travels. The two discover that they are similar. Both are runaways. A runaway's perception of life, is seen through a different prism.

So why are you a Whore?

The sun sets on their 2nd day of travel and as the stage-coach pulls into a rest depot, Bullock and Melvina stretch their legs before the final 120 miles. The Marshal lights a cigar and Melvina notices a 'look' to him. She is accustomed to this look. It shows both interest and fear. She is curious, so she asks

"Something on your mind Marshal?"

"I've been pondering over the last two days, why a woman of your splendor and intelligence is -." She interrupts him.

"A whore," she says. The Marshal stands frozen for a minute and then responds.

"Yes, why no man has sought your hand in matrimony is perplexing Madam Massey," he says.

"You are wrong, sir. Men sought to save me from temptation. Because a woman without a man is a lost soul, wayward in her ways," she says. Her tone edging on spiteful.

"Didn't mean it as an affront to your current condition Melvina. I see you are doing well, peddling flesh, but you are capable of much more," he says and she can read the sincerity and compassion in his eyes.

"I appreciate your candor, sincerity, and compassion

Marshal. However, I am a realist. There are no occupa-
tions for us. They waste our intelligence and ingenuity on
menial tasks of labor, and what jobs there are demands
the constant supervision of a man to ensure that we do it
right each time. No sir, I am done with men deciding my
future, it is time for me to take it on my own," she says.

"Hahaha and in that rebuttal, you provide the irony.
You seek the help of a man," he says with a smirk.

"No, I seek a man who understands the nature of
power. What I do with that information is my issue, Marshal," she says and walks back to the coach. In 10 hours,
they will arrive and that is when the show will begin.

A Meeting of Sorts

The stagecoach pulls into Deadwood and Marshal Seth
Bullock steps out into six inches of mud, urine, feces, and
trash.

"Folks welcome to Deadwood. It's in the middle of
nowhere and nobody's looking," he says and assists Melvina who is ever so happy to have changed into boots.

"How do you stomach the stench?" she asks.

"What stench?"

"Ask and answered Marshal. How far is the Bullock
estate?" she inquires.

"Across town, far from the hustle bustle. My wife should
be back from school. Come hither, these streets are not
safe by any means." The two make their way towards the
Marshal's home a quarter mile up the road.

"When do you suppose I can meet Swearengen?" she
asks as they walk through the crowded streets, full of
people and vulgar language.

"You don't go to meet the devil at night. He is comfortable in that environment; no, we will see him early

tomorrow morning. Besides, Al keeps a sharp eye on the comings and goings of the coaches. He knows you are here. That pig will squirm through the night wondering who you are," Bullock smiles at Melvina, and for the first time, she realizes that a mouth with teeth is underneath his ridiculous mustache.

Melvina enjoys a quiet night with the Bullocks, food, good conversation, and a soft bed. The ingredients for a proper sleep which she needs to prepare for her meeting in the morning. Bullock has a restless sleep, knowing he has arranged no meeting.

The rooster crows early the next morn, and two companions on opposite extremes of the law, head to the man most famous for playing both sides against the middle. Melvina continues to take in the city and its early morning machinations.

"The city that greed and opportunism built," he says. "What are you looking at Miss Melvina?"

"I have never seen so many men condensed in one small place," she says. "I remember Washington during the war. It was never this way," she says and covers her mouth from the foul smell.

"Deadwood is 90% men, and 90% of the women are whores. It's a miracle we have a school, and law," the Marshal says as they arrive at the Gem. "Now you let me do the talking. Al is a crank first thing in the morning," he says.

They enter the Gem and Melvina becomes a topic of discussion. The Marshal requests the proprietor. He finds out Al is still asleep. "Well then wake his short ass up," he says and cautions Melvina not to take a seat just yet. The flunky runs up the stairs, and after five minutes of shouting, Al is rustled out of bed and emerges in a nightshirt tucked into his trousers. He takes one look at Melvina and rushes back to get his jacket. He combs his thick black hair on his way to greet them.

"Well well well, if it isn't the US Marshal and guest. To what do I owe the pleasure of your fucking company at such a God awful time of the fucking day?" he says with a smile to Melvina, but flashes an angry glare towards the Marshal.

"Awww Al quit your bitchin, and I expect a better tone around a proper woman," the Marshal says.

"Proper my fucking ass, I know a whore when I see one," he says. "A right nice one but a whore still the same."

"She is no whore Al. This is Madame Melvina Massey of Fargo," the Marshal says as Melvina bobs a curtsy.

"Oh, so she is the top whore. Simple Tom, where the fuck is my coffee?" he says and offers Melvina and the Marshal a seat away from the other clientele.

"Seth let's get to it, it is way too early in the damn morning for bullshit. So out with it,"

"I was just waiting for the cussin to stop before I presented the lady to you with her proposition," says the Marshal. Swearengen looks up from his coffee cup at Melvina.

"Does she speak, if so I want to hear from her," he says "Now what do you want from me Madam Massey?" he says and takes a sip from the cup.

"Thank you, Marshal," she says. Then looks at Al, "sir it's not what you can do for me, it's what can I do for you?" she says reaching for his cup and then taking a sip.

"Well, I'll be a broke dick millionaire in a town full of whores. What in the fuck can the likes of you do for me?" he says retrieving his cup.

"I offer you balance and a way to keep your establishment and town, free from the WCTU," she says and Swearengen raises an eyebrow to the tone of her response.

"Continue, your last statement has me aroused with

curiosity," he says as the Marshal rolls his eyes and asks for two cups of coffee.

"This territory will break off into two separate states. Wet and dry. That is if we collaborate, otherwise they will both end up dry. The WCTU is well positioned in both Yankton and Bismarck," she says.

"Excuse me as I wish to remain impartial to the politics of the day," says the Marshal, who stands and walks to the Bar.

"What are you thinking, and leave out the parts where I get fucked," he says not hearing but listening to every word Melvina puts forth.

"From what I gather, statehood is fast approaching. The WCTU has assured that North Dakota will be a dry state, however, if that is the case, what's to stop them from then moving South and having both come in as dry states?" Melvina sits back in her chair and watches Al think. She knows a man of his ilk must have surmised the same prophecy.

"Simple Tom, bring me a bottle of whiskey and two glasses. Make sure they are fucking clean," he shouts. "This whore amuses me."

"Could I trouble you for Champagne, Whiskey does not sit well with me," she says. Al pauses for a second leans over and looks Melvina in the eye.

"Who the fuck is you?" he says.

"I am Melvina Massey, and you will assist me in keeping the WCTU at bay in Fargo," she says. Bullock downs a shot of Whiskey and smiles.

"And what if I don't? Why keep the WCTU at bay in Fargo and how does it help either of us? Simple Tom, make that Whiskey and Champagne for Madame." He shouts and lights a cigar.

"I will use what I learn from you over the next two days, and then leverage that knowledge in Fargo to build a better political base. This will ensure that the laws governing the Dakotas are favorable for both of our business endeavors," she says "Ahhh my drink."

"Melvina Massey I can share a few things, but right now your savvy mind has me horny. You're a whore and I'm horny, shall we go upstairs for a poke?" he asks with an evil grin. But, Melvina is focused.

"Sir, I am here on business, not pleasure," she emphasizes.

"And here I thought our business is to please, besides I will pay you for the poke," he says and pours another shot of Whiskey. Melvina considers the proposal and counters.

"Five thousand dollars is what I want," she says.

"I make that in one night," he says.

"Fine, then we will wait until tomorrow morning to consummate that part of the plan. Until then, you keep your dick in your pants and I will keep my pussy wet, agree?" she says and reaches to shake Swearengen's hand.

"Madam Melvina Massey you are one for the books, agreed." A handshake and a shot seal it. Al recounts his travels in various anecdotes that underscore his ability to manipulate any circumstances in his favor.

"Well you don't see that every day," says the Marshal and points to his empty glass for the refill.

"What's that Marshal?" simple Tom asks.

"Al getting fucked by a woman," he says and watches the man pour his drink.

"I guess that depends on what day it is," says Tom.

"See now I know why they call you simple Tom," says the Marshal he finishes his drink and an hour later escorts Melvina back to his home.

Strange Cargo

"Marshal, can I impose on you once more? I want to see the Chinese quarter of the town please," she asks. He looks at her side eyed and gives her an admonishment but complies.

"May I remind you that we are in the 'Badlands'. We call it that for a reason," he frowns. "Sure it's right up the street and to the right, stay close and leave your manners," he says pointing in the direction they are to go.

Chin Kun was the prospective Mayor of the Chinese section of Deadwood. It is a city within a city. The Chinese or 'Celestials' keep to themselves. But, salacious appetites need sinful things. Kun is a provider of such. He runs a brothel with a stable of 25 women age 13- 33. All of whom came to America thinking they were to be brides to rich Chinese men.

"Miss Massey may I ask why in the world are we here?" says the Marshal.

"I am here to string together a proposal and I need you as my protector. Or are you busy?" she asks.

"You know damn well I am not you hurry up the longer we are in the Badlands the more opportunity there is for me to have to shoot someone," he says. She nods in agreement and he leads her to the boss, Mr. Kun.

Melvina is welcomed and as a guest receives tea. Mr. Kun is not so trusting of the Marshal and watches him until he realizes the woman is in charge.

"So how may I be of service to you today?" he says and bows. Melvina does not know what to do, so she bows, and Mr. Kun smiles.

"I see we are in a similar business," she begins.

"What business is that?" he asks.

"The business of lust and sex for a price," she says and Kun looks at the Marshal who assures him he is only here to protect the woman, he hears nothing.

"What will satisfy your tastes today?" Kun says and offers his arm to lead Melvina to another part of his store. The two walk with the Marshal following behind them. There is a narrow hallway with six doors. He says something in Chinese and each door opens to show naked Asian beauties. Melvina is impressed, but they are not what she seeks.

"Is there a senior woman that keeps them in order?" she asks. "Yes I have two since I have two houses to run," he says and calls for the older women, who were once prostitutes too.

"Show me the new ones you have bought," she asks and Kun is surprised, he had underestimated her knowledge. Kun leads Melvina outside the building to a tarp-covered cage, which hides the shame of human trafficked women.

She spends more time here than in the building, Kun notes this. They enter his building and sit for tea. Here Melvina tells the man what she wants.

"I will take two of your girls, one from each house, and not your troublemakers, but the ones that seek more from their confinement," she says and Kun responds.

"You realize that those may be the troublemakers?" he says, Melvina stops in mid stride and sighs.

"Make sure they're not. I require one of your new girls and a minder that speaks English. Cash for the services of four of your women. That is what I want. The price is 1500 dollars; washed, fed and ready to leave in two days. Cash on delivery," she smiles. Melvina's luxurious eyes mesmerize Kun, but he regains his composure and wants to honor her requests.

"This is a good price, what is your name again?" he asks.

"Massey, Melvina Massey," she says and Bullock tips his hat as they exit.

Two days later, after picking Al's brain, Melvina is 5,000 dollars richer and on her way back to Fargo. Swearengen sees great promise in Melvina and wants to send a pimp back with her to help create a more upscale business

in Fargo. But, Melvina's quick wit convinces him otherwise. She has the same intentions.

Mr. Kun receives his payment and two deputies escort the prize possessions to a coach. Melvina bows at the older Chinese woman and says, "Give me 5 years and you can either stay or find your own way," The woman bows and responds,

"I will give you five, but they will do ten," she says.

"Ten why ten, I only require five," Melvina asks.

"Yes ten, it will take you that long to speak and understand our tongue," she smiles.

Melvina returns to Fargo having gained guarded secrets of whore management and politics that old Al never knew he was disclosing.

She sets in motion a course of action that creates strong political alliances for the next 25 years. Some call her methods blackmail or extortion. Melvina has another word for it 'Power'.

Statehood Shenanigans

For three years after her visit to Deadwood, Melvina travels to St. Paul, Chicago, and Bismarck with an entourage of Asian delights and protection from Artemis and an associate of his. She only entertains the highest caliber of clients, wetting their appetites for more in Fargo.

Alliances are made, and her political partners know how best to use her skills of seduction. Three men of great stature within the Republican Party side with proponents of keeping South Dakota wet and North Dakota dry as long as brothels (In North Dakota) can run under the proper fines and inspections. Melvina plays a part in this and other deeds.

Months before statehood, she hosts many of these same affluent men in Moorhead. The hotel's top floor became her own personal bordello of major politics. Negotiated backroom deals, county seats, and future political appointees fall to the tempting lure of sex, provided by Melvina.

The Madame photographs powerful men in compromising positions. Melvina stores the scandalous photos for a more opportune time to use them. The first test will come in 1890 when she secures a loan to buy property for her grand experiment in sexual proclivities called 'The Crystal Palace'.

The Crystal Palace

It is 1890, and now with the full support of powerful investors, Melvina institutes a 'Quid pro quo' style to her Fargo interactions, which culminates with her Crystal Palace. A large six-bedroom two-story house, created with one thing in mind, to leverage her own political ties and keep her criminal enterprise afloat well past statehood. Her allies come from a strange source.

The social elite of Cass and Clay Counties in North Dakota and Minnesota become loyal supporters of Madame Massey. Each receives a hand written (in an elegant calligraphy style) invitation to the grand opening of the Crystal Palace, a place for discrete sexual liaisons.

No beer or alcohol in this North Dakota establishment, a dry state since 1889. Besides, serving whiskey and beer invites a lesser class of customer. Melvina believes she is not bootlegging because she is not distributing or selling her Champagne. It is included in the price of admission, $20 or $30 dollars depending on your preference in sexual perversions. The Crystal Palace is nvite only tonight. Musicians from Kansas City, Chicago, and Washington DC provide the dinner entertainment playing the most popular melodies of the day.

Six pm and the doors swing open for the guests, George Sands leads them into the foyer where they await her formal introduction from Artemis.

"Gentlemen, it is with great pleasure and extreme honor, I Artemis Grant, welcome you to Madame Melvina's Crystal Palace," he says and motions for them to enter the grand parlor. There they find the Asian delights, the mulatto seductresses, and two pale butterflies of French Canadian descent.

The opulence of the parlor impresses the guests. Their hostess awaits. She is standing just below a life-size portrait. Their host adorned in a flowing scarlet red dress, Melvina Massey greets them with a smile.

Dinner service begins at 7pm and the brothel inspectors eat first. Marshal Bullock attends for more of a curiosity than a sexual tryst.

His 'covert' assignment from the Republican party, is to see what politicians Melvina has in her pocket or purse as it were.

Everything is going well, and then a cowboy enters the establishment after nine pm. Standing Bear observes the man and follows him inside to the foyer. The sight of this interloper, who is lost, has Melvina's attention. She excuses herself from two guests and makes her way to the man.

"How may I help you sir?" she says trying not to gag from his scent.

"Is this the Crystal Palace I hear tell about?" he says looking around at the many guests.

"Yes, it is now what brings you here sir?" Melvina asks trying her best to be as polite as possible.

"I am here for a 50 cent poke," he says with a proud smile.

"What the hell you say sir? Listen if you don't get your dirty narrow ass out of here, I will have this half-breed slice you up as if you were a Christmas Goose," she says and then apologizes to Standing Bear. "No 50cent pokes here sir. My butterflies do not screw 100 men a night. We do not serve beer or alcohol and our male customers come pre-washed and have paid their coin for tonight's activities," she says but the cowboy does not move an inch.

"You sure is purdy. Now point me to the man in charge," he says.

"I am the man who runs this place...," she says. "Wait did you wipe your feet?" she asks.

"You ain't no man," he says and then Melvina's head erupts. Standing Bear sees the man's boots and shakes his head he knows what comes next.

"Joseph, Mary, and baby Jesus, you did not track dirt, mud, and shit into this house across my rugs did you?" she says and then looks at George Sands who nods.

George hurls the cowboy out of the Palace and he lands face first into the muddy street. He wipes the mud from his face and sees the man mountain that tossed him.

"Damn they got bears working in here too, I better go somewhere else for a poke," he says and staggers across the road.

Chapter 8

Let us be clear

1901 STATE PENITENTIARY BISMARCK

Political alliances and their current state are not on her mind now. *"Did one of those fools discover my pine box? I need to get word to Artemis and Standing Bear with a quickness but how?"* she thinks and looks over at her cot which promises to be full of critters looking for a host.

Melvina's box has incriminating pictures and documents of the most powerful men in three states. Before arriving in Fargo from Deadwood, she sends a wire to a friend in Chicago who fancies himself as a master of the photographic arts. Her men in Fargo receive a wire too, alerting them of her plans and schedule.

The seduction of power begins in various hotels across four states. Melvina's henchmen arrive a day early at each location. The photographer informs them of his needs and they prepare three rooms for the next night's activities.

Each of her 'girls' provides comfort and sexual services in their own rooms. Every sexual meeting is captured on film. They replicate this in Chicago, St. Louis, Cedar Rapids, St. Paul, and Minneapolis. When Melvina and her entourage arrive in Fargo six weeks later, her crew is seasoned in blackmail.

Her Fargo properties are outfitted in the same manner. When the Crystal Palace opens, each 'butterfly' lives in well-lit ornate rooms. Well-lit rooms for the times, due in part to Fargo having public lighting and electricity to a few properties as early as 1883. A camera sits behind two-way mirrors in each bedroom of the Crystal Palace. The photographer stands in a three-foot crawl space between each of the rooms ready and waiting. As far as the evidence of sexual perversion, she could have used it to negate the bootlegging charges, but thought it better to save it the closer she came to quitting. No matter how sullied her life is, Melvina wants to leave something for her family. This box is that insurance policy.

Time is static as memories of better days flash before her eyes. She realizes her reality in the face of a familiar foe.

"Ahhh my dear back with us I see," he says as Melvina snaps back to her present condition. She feels vulnerable and tries hard not to show fear in the face of the diligent and devious Torsten.

"You still have not said what it is you desire most heinous one," she says, knowing that her tongue is her most powerful weapon now.

"Easy my petulant quim, there's no fun in revealing the grand finale without setting the scene," he says.

"Oh please spare me from your grand delusions of superiority. I made you heel to my wishes with only a pussy promise, now out with it. What do you want?" she says.

"Have you ever considered why two insignificant whores died, or how easy it has been for you to carry so much debt?" he says and waits for this information to hit her. Melvina struggles to reconcile the two separate events.

Her business is lucrative, and she enjoys the benefits of such with her credit. She never considers that her credit came from any other source. Let alone Torsten, who relies on the charity of his father-in-law.

"*Tread with care Melvina, this spider spins a deceptive web, part illusion, part promise, but always lies,*" she ponders before responding.

"The women, every woman in this profession, know the risks of the trade, but enlighten me on the credit that is confusing," she says. Torsten extracts a gold timepiece from his burgundy silk vest. He looks at the watch and then at her.

"I'd love to indulge your curiosity on speculative investments, but I do not have the time. The aim today is to inform you that what you love most, I will destroy just as i have you. Your men will die within the coming hours, your surviving son, will die broke and alone in this frigid land. Because you, Madam Massey refused to cede control of the power you have over men in two counties," he says.

Torsten stands and steps on the remnants of his cigar.

"You will leave them alone, they mean nothing to you," she says, as no other words are available.

"Sit here in this filth and ponder your sins. Commiserate on how your husband sold your secrets to the highest bidder. Reach deep in that feeble mind of yours and realize I own your debt," he reaches into his inner coat revealing deeds, and bills of credit. "My sponsors are your victims. Give me what I want and your stay here is short, trifle with me and it will last every bit of five years and when you return to Fargo, there will only be remorse and pain. Good day Madam Massey," he turns and leaves her to anguish in her thoughts.

Come the Morning

She looks again at the dirty cot and squats near the cell door instead. "When the morning comes, a path will light the way. Bright as your momma's eyes. That's what daddy used to say," she says and hums a hymnal from her youth, and considers how her father is the only man in her life that has not done her wrong. The matron fresh back from wherever she had slithered off to interrupt her thoughts. "Awww isn't this special, a sanctified nigger whore," she says and stands above Melvina, who for the first time, looks in the woman's eyes and sees something compelling. but, she is in no mood for a person in a battle with his or her own self-worth. She has to figure out what Torsten has done. Yet she responds.

"I dare you to say that word again," she says and stands inches from the woman's face. "I dare you,"

"Which do you want to hear, nigger or whore?" the matron says with a seething malice in her tongue. The words do not singe the ears of Melvina. Instead, they open her mind to a reality in front of her.

"Dear child what happened to you, what have men done?" she says, the matron is taken aback and recoils in shame.

"You be quiet and do not speak again, ever you nigger," she says.

"No matter how many times you call me Nigger you don't mean it. There are worse names than Nigger, and I know when a person says it out of fear and out of hurt. Your annunciation is the latter," she says. Melvina abandons her own thoughts and concerns and focuses on the tortured soul in front of her. "What did someone do to you, please I can listen, if you need that," she says. Offering a cup full of compassion to quell the voice of discontent.

The matron sits on a stool at the far end of the dark hallway. "You can't understand, a nigger's mind is too weak to comprehend such things," she says.

"Well then maybe you should stop speaking to niggers and talk to other human beings. There ain't nothing I have seen nor heard in the 'sporting life' that will give me pause. I will listen, now how did they hurt you?" Melvina says one last time hoping to extract something from the woman. No response, she waits and tries once more. "What is your name? You know my name and who I am, nothing to hide here. The craven sexual appetites of men will never surprise me. So I ask you, what is your name, and what have they done to you?" she asks for the last time.

A full half hour passes by before the matron returns to Melvina's cell door. She fights back the tears and the shame long enough to tell Melvina her name. "Thora, my name is Thora Ellisson. I am from St. Paul," she says with no disgust in her voice. "My mother was a domestic for a rich family there. I cannot remember more, other than one day she was there, and the next day she left," she says.

Melvina looks at the woman. Something in her eyes, her hair, and the way she speaks.

"The story goes that my mom came to their employment at an early age as a way to pay off someone else's debt. She served this family for 7 years. One day while the wife was away, the man rapes my mother. He took her every day they say until the wife returned. Months later, I came into this world, and my mother tried her best for two years to care for me, but -." Melvina interrupts her because she knows how this story goes.

"She could not bring herself to care for a white child born out of rape," she says and stands. She faces Thora with a stern look. "This hard life is cruel. Your mother was not a mean person, she was just ill equipped to confront the rest who are," she says.

"There I was alone at three years old, the whites didn't want me, and the niggers they hated me everywhere I went. From home to home, they did the worst things, until one day I up and left those niggers behind," she says as tears stream from her green eyes.

"How did you survive?" Melvina asks knowing the answer to this question.

"I passed as soon as I could get out of St. Paul and to Minneapolis, I passed. I continued into the Dakotas and Bismarck, passing myself off as white. No one is the wiser," she says as her hard and defiant demeanor returns.

"Do I remind you of the people that did you wrong?" Melvina asks of the woman.

"I see an elegant and proud woman, someone accomplished despite her odds. But, most I see me. A nigger who is passing and I despise you," she says.

"Why do you despise me, what have I done to you? I am not the one who treated you wrong or did you harm in your youth. Why am I the brunt of your hate?" she says. Melvina steps away from the cell door.

"I hate you because you are everything I want for myself but every time I look into a mirror I see a nigger," she says.

"Thora they call that self-hate and self- loathing, neither of which will ever bring you peace. You need to stop passing and live. Do you think I tried to pass? Oh no dear, I let folks think what they want to think and then control how they will always see me," she says. "So your mother's employer rapes her and you are the result. She tries but ends up abandoning you, the white people do not want you, and the black folks treat you worse than a dog. That's behind you now. What lies in front of you? A new story if you write it," she says and sits leaving Thora to her thoughts and her reality.

"You make it sound so easy," she says from a distance.

"Life is no easy trick. Men are difficult to understand. Most are dumb, but it's the stupid ones that will break your heart every time. People are cruel in every way," she says as her head falls into her hands.

Chapter 9

The Years of Love and Lies

1863-75 WASHINGTON D.C.

A young woman named Henrietta Massey spends much of her 20s traversing between Falls Church Virginia, and DC where she is a socialite and desired by many men. She works as a care provider in city hospitals caring for the many wounded soldiers returning from the battlefields. It is during this service that her life is forever changed.

One day in 1864, a young Henrietta passes three Union Soldiers a block from her place of employment, The Armory Square Hospital, in SW DC. The soldiers yell out mild flirtatious things to her but she is oblivious. She assumes that they do not know her true ethnicity, and this keeps her safe. She thought.

The penalties for sexual misconduct are strict on both sides. But, harassment of black and Native American women by white soldiers, and by harassment I mean rape. This sexual misconduct goes unpunished by Union and Confederate forces.

Her shift ends at 1700 (5pm) and once again, the soldiers are positioned one block away from the Hospital. She is leery of them but does not believe they mean her any harm, just men behaving like boys. Other women made the same mistake. She continues on her way and they try to gain her attention. Watching the entire scene from a distance is a young Negro named Artemis.

The Army of the Potomac uses him as a scout. Artemis grew up near Richmond, but often travelled and hunted in various areas of Virginia and Maryland with his master, who upon his death freed young Artemis and his mother.

The soldiers are trying to convince Henrietta to join them for drinks and conversation in 'Murder Bay', east of the White House on the Pennsylvania Ave side.

Murder Bay is notorious for brothels, saloons, and murder. This is not a place for young Henrietta but she decides that one drink will not hurt. Dusk approaches and she agrees to join them.

However, one soldier removes a flask full of Whiskey, and seduces her into taking a few drinks. She agrees, feeling on the adventurous side tonight, but not too adventurous as to be in a public space drinking alcohol. So the group ducks into a tight alley near Murder Bay to take a few swigs.

One stands lookout as the others drink with Henrietta. She takes her second turn at the flask and before she knows it, one man delivers a blow to the back of her head; she falls forward hitting her forehead on the adjacent brick wall. The world is spinning, but she makes out the shapes of the soldiers as they descend upon her. Ripping her garments top and bottom to gain access to her private parts, so surreal, but her reality is a rape in progress. The men fumble with her undergarments, and she regains her wits. Young Henrietta lashes out at one and receives a punch to the face.

"Willie she scratched me! Fuck this cunt and let's put a bullet in her," he said, leering at Henrietta.

"No we will fuck her and then slice her up, less noise that way," says the senior of the three. He produces a knife.

Artemis arrives and shoves a knife in the neck of their lookout. Henrietta fears for her life and receives another punch to the head which knocks her unconscious. She does not hear Artemis call out to her 'Melvina' nor does she see him shoot the other two deviants.

Two hours later, she regains her wits and awakens to the sounds of a piano, light conversation, and the most comfortable sheets she has ever felt.

"Where am I, am I in heaven?" she says aloud.

"Only if there is a high-class brothel in heaven, but I doubt that," a voice says. She will later discover that the voice was the proprietor 'Mary Ann Hall' who tends to her wounds.

"What is this place, who brought me here, I heard shots -." She rambles on of the incident as Ms. Hall and Artemis listen.

"You heard shots, yes, but it's Murder Bay, there are always shots. No one heard, and if they did, no one cared," Miss Hall says. "Artemis saw how the men pursued you, and knew it had the makings of trouble," she says.

"I have no words for their kind. They lure women into Murder Bay and rape them. A few escape, others are gobbled up by that place," he says "But not you Melvina."

"Who is Melvina and why is he calling me that name?" Henrietta asks.

"His mother was a mulatto; she worked for me after arriving in the city. Men attack her near Murder Bay only three months after their arrival here. Artemis witnesses the entire scene. He has worked for me and the Army after the war starts. I guess you remind him of her, there is a slight resemblance," she says wiping Henrietta's forehead.

A full day of rest ensues and Miss Hall returns to the bedside of Miss Massey and makes her an offer. She suggests that the young woman stay as long as she likes, but she will have to earn her keep. Hall explains and identifies the jobs as cleaning, cooking, and other domestic duties. The pay is minimal, and she will share a communal room in the basement with eight other workers. Or, she could become a 'butterfly' of the house. Which means she gets a room and clothes and other privileges.

"You are a rare breed and my clientele pays good coin; they love the lure of Negro women but are more attracted to the mulatto or quadroon. I always provide for my customers and they pay a heavy price for the luxury. It is $25 to enter. And $50 for an all-night poke with my butterflies. We only serve champagne, and each liaison comes with dinner, another $10 though. Yes, no fifty cent fucks here my sweet. So, think it over. But come dawn, you are cooking or fucking, your call," she says with a smile.

Henrietta takes a minute to decide that the sporting life is for her. She calls out to Miss Hall... "Why wait until morning, I will be a butterfly, and you can call me Melvina, Melvina Massey," Within two months of joining, she becomes a mainstay of the establishment three blocks from the Capitol steps. Madam Hall took a liking to the young seductive mulatto, and convinces her that if she plays her cards right, she might marry a prominent officer or politician. Both appealing thoughts to Melvina during the war years. Melvina is the 'bait'. The reputable men crave her. But, the price is steep, anywhere from $100–200 dollars. However, one man wins the bidding war and Melvina's heart.

Minnesota Congressmen, Darrel P.H.'Chance' Gorman, was a 2nd Lieutenant in the courageous First Minnesota Volunteer Infantry Regiment, which held Cemetery Ridge at Gettysburg. Gorman becomes a Major in 1864 and meets Melvina for the first time. Both are smitten, but Gorman returns to Minnesota after the war. He comes back to DC in 1868 as a first-term congressional representative and resumes their courtship. They take trips to Chicago, New York, and Philadelphia, and no one ever suspects she is a black woman.

JUNE 1875

Three years later and one year into the representative's third term, he asks for her hand in marriage forgetting he has a wife back in St. Paul. Melvina is living in Chicago when she finds out his real status. Once discovered, Melvina demands Gorman get an annulment, but he calls off their nuptials instead. This infuriates Melvina who then writes the wife. She exposes the sordid details of the affair and the husband's appetite for sexual perversions. Oral sex in the 1870-1900s, is a sexual perversion.

Melvina returns to DC and continues her harassment of the wife. The scandal gets out of hand. Darrel P.H. Gorman takes Melvina to court in DC, to stop the harassment. As he testifies, she gives him the coldest stare, one of loathing and pure hate. During a recess, she hurls accusations and lewd remarks towards the wife.

"He is a coward and a liar, and you are a sorry heifer. I hope his penis rots inside of you," she screams.

"Well as a whore I am sure you know a rotten one when you see one," says the wife.

Melvina's attorney ushers her into the street for air.

"Calm yourself, this won't do us any good if the judge hears of this little escapade, so please stifle your emotions," he says. But Melvina can only see vengeance through her crystal blue eyes.

"I want his gonads in a sling Winston. His lying ass needs to pay," she says. Her attorney thinks on it for a second.

"You are right. The chances of this affair ruining him back home are slim. However, listen to me..." he says and pulls her close. "I will inform the Judge that we will patch this up and move on. Then tomorrow I will file a 'Breach of Promise' suit against him and his estate," he says smiling and feeling proud of himself.

"Winston you think I can win such a thing?" she asks.

"I am under retainer from your employer, and I don't come cheap. When I say, I can get you satisfaction believe it. Need two witnesses that knew of your nuptials and were privy to the entire affair. Now then, we will ask for $5,000 hoping to get anywhere from $100-250 dollars.

Will that be enough gonad squeezing for you?" he asks.

"Fuck no. He needs to learn not to toy with a woman's heart. No, $500 is the least I will settle for," she says, still red with fury.

"Said and done. Let us make haste and settle this other matter first," he says.

They enter the courtroom and Winston Comfort, heads for the opposing attorney. The attorneys talk. Melvina looks forward, not turning her head left, or right. Gorman's attorney discusses the matter with his clients and they agree. Both Lawyers shake hands and the Judge notified of their decision. He adjourns with the parties having agreed to part ways. The judge finds the representative's actions were dubious, and scolds Melvina for her actions in the lobby of the court. Case adjourned.

The next day Melvina's attorney files a suit against Gorman for 'Breach of Promise', A two-day trial ensues and the parties settle for $250.00 resolution which soothes Melvina's rage but does not include the court costs. The judgement (covered in the papers and in the court record) never reflects closure of any kind. It states that Melvina drops the case. They report Gorman as a 'messenger' not a member of Congress. He leverages favors from the war to keep his name out of the papers and out of court documents. Gorman, and the man she meets two years later in Chicago, Henry Rae, forever taint Melvina's trust in men.

All Men are not Equal

Melvina returns to Chicago after her scandalous battles with Congressman Gorman. She resumes her work at a makeshift laundry house. A sign says 'M&M Laundry Specials' but in the back three rooms, tricks are turned by four whores Melvina 'manages'.

M&M Laundry Specials has been in business since Melvina and Artemis arrive in 1874. Artemis maintains order, and her niece (Maggie Massie) assists in the front room charade. The laundry is a fraud but the occasional new customer comes in to drop a load. Artemis or Maggie give the person a receipt and then hustle over to the Chinese launderer four blocks south.

Melvina charges five times the price which often scares off those 'not knowing' consumers. The outlandish price restricts her clients to repeat customers and referrals.

"Artemis do you ever miss DC?" asks Maggie as she re-arranges towels that have sat in the same spot for two months.

"Yes, I do. I miss the trees and crabbing in the spring," he says and then looks at her folding the towels. "Maybe you should wash those towels instead of folding em," he says.

"What in the hell for?" she says.

"Well someone, someday, might just look at them and notice how dirty they are," he says.

"Like I care, you and I both know men do not come in here for laundry," she says and continues folding the dusty towels. A man walks in with a bag of clothes as Melvina arrives from the backroom.

"Good morning, I have a load I need back by Thursday if you please. Shirts with light starch and pressed," the man says and the three Virginia natives do not move or speak. "Uh hello," he says again.

"Hello sir, what can we do for you?" Melvina asks as Maggie and Artemis look on in disbelief.

"You didn't hear what I said? I saw you standing right here when I said it," he says.

"Yes I heard you but I did not understand what you wanted," she says. Artemis suspects the customer is a police officer in disguise. Maggie says nothing but her big green eyes lock in on her aunt.

"Oh so if you heard me then what's so hard to understand?" he says drawing the frustration out of Melvina who rolls her eyes at the man and opens the door leading to the back rooms. She stops in the doorway and asks...

"Sir why are you here, I mean are you lost?" she asks.

"I'm here to get my laundry done, this is a laundry isn't it?" he asks and then grabs one of the dusty towels. "Not a clean one," he says and Artemis laughs aloud.

"See didn't I tell you, haha," Artemis laughs. Maggie's cheeks turn red with shame.

"Ladies can you show yourselves so this man knows what we sell in here," Melvina shouts. The women step out from the three rooms, dressed in undergarments. "This is M&M Laundry and Specials. These are the specials," she says. Three café au lait toned Negro women, tall, short, thick, and slim walk up to Melvina, but not out into the main room.

"My God," the man says. "Is this a..."

"Brothel, that's the word," she says. "However, we can do your laundry for $10. The price is $5 but you get a poke for $5 too. I find that to be reasonable don't you?" she says with a smile.

"This is an abomination. You cannot move me towards sin you high 'yella' jezebel," he says. Both Maggie and Artemis know what is coming next. Melvina is as patient as Job but has a temper.

"Sir, before I call you out your name let me ask you two questions. Did you or did you not read the damn sign as you entered this place of business? The sign that says 'M&M Laundry and Specials, one bag $10' Do you recall reading that sign sir?" she asks.

"Uh yes I remember reading the sign," he says.

"Uh huh, so you read a sign advertising cleaning services 20 times the going rate and you still walked in? Who does that? You gonna pay $10 to have your laundry done when it's only 50 cents across the street?" she says.

Melvina's 'specials' turn and walk back to their rooms. She closes the door behind them.

"So what are you, a pastor, reverend, father, or a Bishop?" she asks.

"Reverend Haskell and I -,"

"No need to apologize. They all come through these doors. Catholics, Protestants, Methodists, and

Anglicans you name it. So are you going to drop your laundry off and leave, or are you going in the back?" she asks. The Reverend huffs and walks out of the store. He returns to grab the laundry bag and leaves.

"Well ain't that something huh Melvina, we won't see him again," Maggie says.

"No we will see him again; he took the receipt so he knows where to come. He will be back, they always come back," she says.

Reverend Haskell hurries back to his sponsor, Boss Gates. He walks seven long blocks never suspecting that Artemis is following and arrives at the 'Pork Pit' tired and sweaty. Gates is busy seasoning a pork butt in the kitchen. Dinner is in four hours so time is a commodity.

"You should exercise more Rev. The distance between the two businesses is not that long. Give me the details and be on your way," he says.

"There are tainted women there, for sure," the Reverend says. He pats his face with a handkerchief. Nervous and eager to leave.

"How many women Rev," asks Gates. He shoves the pork butt in a smoker and waits.

"I only saw four, but that hi yella Jezabel in charge, is something else," he says.

"How so Rev?"

"She is bossy and condescending and has a viper's mouth," he says. Gates smiles and stacks five silver dollars on a table.

"You can leave now Rev and don't mention this to anyone," says Boss Gates. The Reverend takes the coins and leaves without a word.

"What chu think Henry and keep it short. I gotta put sauce on these ribs," he says. A man dressed in dandy fashion steps forward.

He is 30, with a slight build, and racially ambiguous. His name is Henry Rae, but most people believe that is fake. A pimp, gambler, loan shark and not good at any of it.

"I am curious, is your intention to home in on her enterprise or to teach her a lesson?" he asks.

"Henry I'm asking the fucking questions young buck and I already told you to keep it short. I want to know your thoughts on her obvious disregard for how I do business," Gates says.

"Boss, I doubt that filly from Virginny even knows you exist. But I will investigate this myself, and demand our usual 35%," Henry says.

"So now you give my money away too, you know damn well it's 50% off the top Henry," he says and mops the ribs with sauce.

"If she is as good looking as she is bossy, I will discount her my 15%," Henry says smiling as he leaves.

"Damn mulattoes he knows God damn well he only gets 5%," says Gates. He shoves the ribs into the smoker.

Artemis sees the Reverend leave, and another person follows. He notes his stature, dress, and walk. Artemis follows Henry Rae to M&M with a growing rage filling his being. Or is it distrust?

Chapter 10

And then there is Henry Rae

The ubiquitous mendacious Henry Rae enters Melvina's life when she is at her most vulnerable. This Boss Gates low-level pimp from the Midwest schemes on her money and emotions squandering both. But, Melvina always lets him back in for reasons only known to her and God.

They meet in Chicago after Melvina returns from her court battles in Washington. Henry notices her expensive and extravagant tastes. Which means she is a white socialite wanting to play on the 'dark side of town' or she is mulatto.

He moves in and charm wins the day over good judgment, however, Melvina plays him for a while, because she has big plans for Minnesota and the gold in the 'Plains States'. Plans that do not involve Henry yet.

Henry is a mulatto passing as white. He will be Melvina's well-kept pet until something better. Melvina keeps him in new shoes and clothes, and he can always sweet-talk her when he is caught cavorting with 'sporting girls'. He should know better than to test his fortune. That is Henry Rae though, carefree and a real jerk.

But, his taste for having 'his cake' catches up to him in Chicago, and that is where Melvina leaves him in 1879. She heads to Minnesota and tries to put together her next moves. After six months, Melvina Massey moves forward with her plans to open multiple brothels in a booming town. By 1890, she owns four brothels and is building another one.

A year after Melvina opens the Crystal Palace, who shows up in Fargo but none other than Henry Rae. He never changes his ways but marries Melvina in the 1893. Henry then disappears for three years, amassing debt in Chicago, which brings him back to Fargo in 1899, where he aligns himself with those that want to end the mulatto Madame's grip on local politics and commerce.

Two No Good Men

Ten years since statehood and the Red River Valley is booming. Agriculture and cattle make the state very wealthy. Yet the need for nocturnal sinful acts still grips the twin cities of Fargo and Moorhead. One for prostitution, the other booze. Anika Marlowe and her WCTU is successful in keeping North Dakota dry, but, the machinations of Melvina Massey ensures that prostitution will be in Cass County until the turn of the century.

So, the WCTU turns its sights towards women's suffrage issues and works to liberate and baptize the wanton wayward whores of the Hollow. The men of Cass County dislike their change in strategy. Their rebuke is strong and swift. The WCTU receives a serious blow to their suffrage work and many do not pick up the cause of Christian charities until later around 1910.

With his wife's sole purpose in Fargo now diminished to just domestic duties, and her ability to galvanize citizens to a cause gone, Torsten assumes a bigger and harsher role in the household. Torsten has spent the last decade maneuvering in Cass county political circles, deciding to be a kingmaker and not a king. His main issue is that the Crystal Palace remains the prime location for such wheeling and dealing. He decides on another course of action one that will remove the Palace from the playing field, allowing for a more discreet and 'white' lodge to gain prestige.

Torsten puts his plan into play but first he must flex his muscles on the home front where his controlling nature has stifled and smothered the once vibrant and energetic Anika. Now Torsten moves to strengthen his position as the true head of the household.

He tries to wrestle more of his wife's money held in trust, but her father's lawyers are not impressed or deceived. They only approve a stipend of $100 a month for the home and its upkeep. This outrage embarrasses Torsten who then beats a whore in the Hollow. Something he is more prone to do of late, now that the Crystal Palace and any other brothel owned and operated by Melvina Massey is off limits.

It is during this time in 1896 that the ever scheming Torsten eavesdrops on a conversation between bankers in a Moorhead pub. They are voicing regrets stemming from the great panic of 1893, which rips through the stock market and country, causing railroads and banks to collapse overnight. The information comes to Torsten that none other than J.P. Morgan will assume control of the bankrupt Northern Pacific Railroad.

He knows the first rule of power, knowledge, and hurries to make a call. Torsten uses what money he has to buy a new suit and a ticket to visit his father-in-law back east. Torsten negotiates the following contract: a positive return on the information he gives ensures him of 20% of the profits. Any negative returns over the agreed-upon period, and he will grant his wife a divorce. The father-in-law jumps at the offer, but his lawyers are skeptical of Torsten. For two hours the bankers and lawyers make discreet inquiries and satisfied with their findings approve of the offer on the table.

Torsten now waits as Mr. Ernest Inge, makes many purchases in most J.P. Morgan holdings to include the Northern Pacific. Speculating that more investors will do the same, he gets in early when the prices are low. When the official announcement comes, the share prices in the railroad triple. Torsten has what he always wanted, his own money.

This does not bode well for his wife in Fargo, who soon after becomes a shell of the once virtuous and enterprising woman that stepped off the train in 1881. Their home becomes a suppressive existence for her and the two girls coming into womanhood. The example Torsten gives is not one of a loving father and caring husband. He controls every piece of their lives right to the clothes they wear.

The shift in power has damaged the family dynamic, and even the younger boys treat the women of the house with disrespect and contempt. Dysfunction is hereditary, but the cycle can be broken if one is bold enough to set the proper boundaries. Anika Marlowe once held the moral high ground. But even a virtuous woman can fall victim to her carnal desires. In the fall of 1892, Anika tires of Torsten the whoremonger, whose public disrespect (although Melvina had long since dismissed him in 1887) had grown out of control. She acts on her own lustful thoughts.

Anika is no saint though her own discretions and secret meetings with the young pastor, although not carnal, are still lewd in intent. One evening, she visits the pastor unannounced and without warning and is shocked to see he has another WCTU member willing to give him what he lusts for without reservation.

This is not only a blow to her heart, but her ego, as she thinks 'How many more members of the WCTU have fallen prey to his lurid cravings? Worst yet, do any know of my own dalliances with the devil?' She retreats to her home and from public view in shame.

Torsten suspects the pastor from the beginning and sticks the proverbial knife deeper into his wife's heart, commanding her obedience now out of guilt and shame. However, not even these resounding wins in his personal life can assuage his maniacal machinations over Melvina. So he heads to a seedy brothel in the Hollow to think. The madam sends a bottle of whiskey over to Torsten who recognizes another visitor.

'My eyes deceive me, but I could swear this man in front of me is none other than Henry Rae, Melvina's husband, or consort' he ponders and continues to watch the well-dressed man at the far end of the room. Torsten calls for the madam and inquires if he is indeed Henry Rae. She confirms his identity and Torsten sends over a complimentary drink.

The two toast each other and within a few minutes, Henry Rae joins a man who has schemed against Melvina's interests for at least a decade. He has tried to intimidate her, to no avail, he has attempted to win her over in the bed, but she turns him out instead. Torsten has failed at every turn because he did not have power, and as we have discussed, knowledge is power.

"Good evening what brings a man of your station to this dive," Henry says pouring himself a shot of whiskey.

"What I do and where I go is my business and mines alone. But to answer your question, your wife has seen fit to ban me from other areas of the Hollow," he says.

"Well I am sure you earned your eviction, but then again, when dealing with Melvina one never knows their true position in her life until she dismisses you," Henry downs his shot and pours another.

"So can I presume this happened to you?" Torsten says fishing for information.

"Your presumption is accurate sir," "Isn't that something and here you are newlyweds," Torsten says.

"So what of you, what brings you here?" he asks and helps himself to another drink. Torsten is watching him, waiting for the liquor to take control of the man's senses.

"I am here for the usual poke, but these whores are of low quality, so the illegal drink is sufficient," both men know that a few nights in jail faces them if the law bolts through the doors. Alcohol is only available in Moorhead, just across the bridge. The two men continue their commensuration and conclude that a woman needs a lesson in humility. Torsten smiles in agreement and waits to hear what Henry Rae is ready to tell him.

"She is black? How do you know this, and can it be proven beyond a shadow of a doubt?" he says in a low voice. Henry leans in and discloses even more.

"Oh there's that but that alone won't make her heel, her smuggling in booze from Moorhead, now that is something a prosecutor will want to hear," he says pointing to his empty glass. Torsten fills it and asks for more details.

"There are tunnels underneath the Palace that lead to other areas in Fargo. These are her distribution points. There are four of them," he says.

Mr. Torsten Marlowe cannot believe what he is hearing and who is delivering it. He asks for more information. Henry sheds light on a mystery that occurred in 1891. The arson of the 1st Crystal Palace under suspicious circumstances. A drunk man perished in those flames. Henry was an acquaintance of Mr. Williams and is present at the fire.

"Who killed him Henry?" asks Torsten. "Was it Melvina or did she have one of her minions do it?"

"Melvina is many things but a woman who dispatches her men on homicidal missions is not one of them," he says.

"Fair enough. The fire?" Torsten senses a reluctance in Henry, so he presses him harder.

"This fire and murder are complicated things to discuss. I do not want to implicate myself or others -."

"So you seek 'cover'?" he asks.

"No amnesty is more in line," Henry says.

"For the murder or the fire?" Torsten asks. Henry seeks to hide his own participation in the crime by being as vague as possible. But, Torsten wants details.

"I met Melvina in Chicago around 1875. My purpose in establishing a relationship with her is business. My boss required that she pay for the privilege of whoring in his part of town, and I served as his emissary," he says.

"Go on."

"This business arrangement starts off rocky but over two years proves profitable for both parties. Boss Gates invests more in Melvina and sponsors her endeavors in other cities. Until she disappears around 1879. I find her in St. Paul in 1886, and we resume a short romance," he says. Torsten's face contorts in anguish.

"You are boring me, Mr. Rae," he says.

"My sponsor comes on hard times and insists that I retrieve the money he is due from Melvina. A task I was unsuccessful in accomplishing because she was no longer in St. Paul. I discover her whereabouts in Fargo and show up at the grand opening of the Palace. You realize that I was not welcome one bit. Artemis threatened me frequently," he says.

"Artemis? I never took him to be more than just show," says Torsten.

"Mr. Marlowe, believe me when I say, Artemis Grant is more than meets the eye. He is a killer and one to approach with extreme caution. If one plans the demise of Melvina Massey, they best start with Artemis," he says. Torsten makes a mental note and bids him continue.

"I am granted permission to speak with the Madam and warn her of my bosses intentions. She dismisses me with a warning to not return. One month later after receiving orders from my sponsor, I set out to send her a message. A fiery one." Torsten grins because he knows how this will play out.

"So you set the fire but did not count on the drunk negro being in the building," he says.

"No sir, Williams was my accomplice. We both were drinking in Moorhead building up the courage for the task. When we arrived, no one was present, and he set the fire. Artemis discovers us and his shots find their mark. I escape without further detection," Henry says.

"This is good information and I will devise a way to use it without implicating the source. I now have the leverage to turn politicians to my cause," he says. The two men toast in agreement. Torsten and Henry Rae strike up a contract and become partners in the demise of Melvina because such a thing has a superb price. The total cost of the betrayal is $10,000 dollars, which the two men split.

So what is the big news that will seal her doom? That she is a bootlegger in open defiance of the State's prohibition laws. This is a meaningless assertion since Melvina has always operated her establishment in the open with nothing to hide. If they wanted to charge her with bootlegging, they could have done so over the years 1889-1900, but they did not.

Bootlegging in North Dakota often resulted in a fine and no jail time.

The new information Torsten combines with the level of her criminal enterprise (to include murder) might prove disturbing. He is counting on this and that she is a Negro, to offend their sensibilities. Torsten admires her cunning and ability to hide her truth. Yet he questions if this is an example of her power or the town not enforcing the law? No matter the reasons, Melvina is a victim of it all to include her own hubris.

Henry Rae provides her enemies with the essential proof she is a Negro and that she played the entire town. Supported by the politicians, newspapers launch a derogatory campaign on her reputation in the region. Most town folk know of her efforts after the flood and her accommodating a Norwegian church by allowing them to tap into her water feed. She pays for their water too. But the goodwill from moral folks fades when they discover that the grand Madame is a Negro who has sold alcohol in her establishments in direct defiance of the law.

Henry Rae provides the evidence to support these accusations in the press. Besides his own testimony, he provides pictures of him and Melvina's marriage ceremony in Minnesota. Where Negro members of his family surround the couple, inferring that one or both of them are Negro. Henry does not dispute he is half-black, so at the worst, Melvina is a white woman who has married a black man. But, most assume she is not white because no white woman marries a black man. So now they are presented with a choice of which offends their sensibilities more. Many raids in the Hollow follow and expose a busy network of tunnels between her properties to move the booze and customers. They suspect more are available.

Anika Marlowe and the WCTU do not revile in the demise of Melvina Massey, instead, they bear witness to a powerful woman's fall. The die cast, the charges filed, her appeal lost.

Melvina Massey is now a convicted felon, for bootlegging. She is only the second person to be charged and convicted of this crime in the states history. And no other citizen receives this justice before the end of prohibition 30 years later. But her true crime (in their eyes) was being a Negro and not telling anyone. Melvina is cornered but not beaten.

Chapter 11

Truth and what You Believe

1901 BISMARCK PENITENTIARY

At the dawn of the second day of her sentence, Melvina is nervous in her cell. She paces back and forth still upset over Torsten's visit she has not slept. Now the years slip through her face unveiling her true age for the moment. It is 6am, and she sits on the floor. The pause from the nonstop pacing gives her body a welcomed respite. She falls asleep. Four hours pass and Melvina is still asleep, now in a huddled mass on the floor. Thora passes the cell three times allowing her to continue resting. The only other noise in the women's space occurs two hours later with arrivals of another prisoner and a visitor.

Seth Bullock arrives all the way from his ranch near Deadwood, to confirm a truth. He sits on a stool in front of her cell, searching her physical features. Seth is looking for proof of a truth he is trying to disprove.

"Good morning sunshine, but for accuracy, it is more around noon than morning," he says as he removes his hat.

"Hello Marshal, what brings you to this place of forgotten things?" she asks and apologizes for her clothing and hair.

"I am here to verify if it is true," he says.

"What lies need defending Marshall?" she asks.

"Are you a Negress yes or no?" he asks leaning closer to her cell.

"Oh, that is a truth," she says.

"How is this possible?" he says now standing.

"Deception is a truth within a lie. But, I never lied, I never thought it in my best interest to correct a town's perceptions," she says and then stretches. "But no man of your station comes by this way to assist a 60-year-old whore, black or white. What brings you here Marshal?" Melvina's quick wit returns and now she seeks to remove the cloudiness of the past evening.

"Well since you can prove a negative, and I am speaking to my doubts of your race, which you have now confirmed. Now I need to know something else, something to do with your political connections," he says pulling a matchstick from his vest pocket and using it to pick his teeth.

"You are the second man to come here in 48 hours seeking such information. Yet here I sit in filth. Doesn't seem as though anyone wants to make a woman comfortable as a show of sincerity,"

"Sincerity my ass, as sure as you're born, these men will see you swinging from a tree. There's a specter, unsavory, reckless and racist, easing its way into the Dakotas," he says.

"Go on you have my attention," she says.

"Well good, my friends of the Republican Party want to ensure that what you have is in safe keeping. How is that for expanding your attention?" he says and flicks the match away. "I see, they send you for confirmation but offer no other assurances? Typical, men wanna be on top but do not understand what it means to ride," she says with the sexual innuendo well received. "Mm

"I see, they send you for confirmation but offer no other assurances? Typical, men wanna be on top but do not understand what it means to ride," she says with the sexual innuendo well received.

"Mm hmmm Madame Melvina what assurances do you need? Oh and keep in mind I am still in law enforcement," he leans up against the wall that separates each cell. "Now only we know what you need," he says.

"My men, I want them safe, and then I want out of this dank ass cell. Somewhere, anywhere than this," she says.

"And..."

"The information is safe...for now. Someone else seeks the same insurance policy, and he is not playing fair," Melvina seeks to push her upper hand a tad more, hoping to include her debt too. But, Seth does not budge.

"I believe we have an accord, Madame Massey. The rest will need to wait until your release. I leave you now in the care of the warden who is a good man and prison reformer," he tips his hat and leaves.

1901 FARGO

George Sands leaves the Crystal Palace at 9pm, to check on the other brothels. Two blocks from his first stop, a teen runs by him and steals his hat.

"Why you little fuck, drop it, drop it right now I say," he screams and gives chase. The boy runs fast, a George Sands of 20 years ago could have caught him by now.

But, the 55yo man finds it hard to keep pace. The boy vanishes just before the North Dakota side of the bridge. George leans over, grabs his knees, to catch his breath. That is when he sees them. Four brutish men carrying large sticks, descend upon him.

"Oh it's a party you want is it, cmon let's begin the dance," he shouts and the men advance upon him. George waits for the first aggressor to reach him and then fires off a hard right jab, splitting the board and the man's nose. The others begin their attacks with fury, pummeling the large man. George responds with a hurricane of ferocious punches and kicks that break limbs and jaws. In less than three minutes his adversaries are done.

"That's what comes to those who piss off George Sands," he says and turns into a rifle barrel. One shot to center mass, staggers him, two more men join in with handguns. Six shots bring the man to his knees but the last shot from behind kills the mountain. They find his body the next morning on the Moorhead side of the river.

1901 BISMARCK PENITENTIARY

Melvina spends the rest of her day in idle chatter with the woman in the adjacent cell. She is serving a five-year sentence for theft and debts she cannot pay. Which strikes Melvina as odd since one is a result of the other.

"But how is she to pay off her debt in jail? That makes no sense, she could have sold pussy for two years and called it a day," she thinks and wonders two things. She wants out of this place and 'when will this woman stop with her incessant bitching about her money?'

A similar problem faces Melvina if she cannot outsmart Torsten. So she thinks.

The morning arrives and with it another visitor. It is none other than Mrs. Anika Marlowe. The aging evangelical still cloaked in black sits across from her nemesis of 20 years. But, she does not come to gloat; she came out of respect for what Melvina is and to deliver terrible news. Another dawn and Melvina finds herself ensnared in the motivations of white folk once again.

This woman needs what the great Madame Massey can offer. This meeting could never have been possible if it were not for a thawing in their relationship and a cease-fire of sorts in the late 1890s.

Anika succumbs to the fever after the great flood of 1897. Melvina comes to her bed and nurses her back to health, despite Torsten's objections. His demented mind only sees the opportunity for wealth, a dead wife, and four grandchildren will clinch a healthy inheritance. A slight in his delusional mind. But, a debt Anika's children will never forget.

Melvina is a success because people always underestimate her fortitude and her ability to seize opportunity from the grasp of despair.

"To what do I owe this pleasure, first Torsten and now you, what in blazes is going on in Fargo?" Melvina asks. Mrs. Marlowe is slow to respond but when she does the news hits Melvina harder than a punch to the gut.

"Your man, the big one, he met a savage and brutal end. They found him yesterday morning on the Moorhead side of the river," she says head bowed. Melvina stammers to a response.

"And...the others, what of them?" she asks.

"Artemis escaped a gun attack at the Palace. Someone waited until he exited the house and shot at him, hitting his hat and the frame of the door. I have no news of the Indian," she says and Melvina's face turns pale. Her only hope was for her men to send word to associates but now she has no clue if they are dead or alive. How to work this woman?

"I need to impose on your charity and understanding this morning for I am in need of a big favor," Anika says and for the first time in 20 years, Melvina can see her true soul.

"My daughter is on the cusp of ruining her life and she is beyond reason," Anika says as she details how her daughter desires to work for the Madam of Fargo. Melvina listens to the evangelical speak of a rebellious daughter and mother conflict. However, she recognizes what it must have taken this moral and upright woman to come all this way to beg for help.

"Anika I sense a change in you, I noticed it first when you were sick. The will to live had left your soul you were a beaten and demoralized woman. I knew of the pastor and his dirty deeds..." she says and watches as Anika squirms in her seat, the entire escapade still has an effect on her. "He enjoyed the 'tunnels', more than most. Torsten is an absolute ass. Not unusual for him to work your ill-advised sexual tryst to his gain," Melvina stops her observations

---

The Color of Power

there because an epiphany has shown itself to her.

She agrees to help Anika with her middle daughter. First...

"There is something you can do for me, I need you to deliver a message to Artemis and Standing Bear. Just tell them 'the time is now'," she says. "They will do the rest." Melvina smiles and Anika thanks her before leaving. The meeting lasts only 20 minutes. Thora walks over to Melvina's cell, keeping her eye on Mrs. Marlowe as she walks out of the wing.

"She is not trustworthy, at least the other two told you what they wanted, she was lying from the moment she walked in," she says.

"Yes," Melvina says in response and then "When I am released you should come visit me, I may have something for you to do," she says and returns to her seat on the floor.

I never liked that Woman

1901 BISMARCK PENITENTIARY

Anika Marlowe exits the penitentiary and enters a waiting carriage.

"Well, what did she say?" asks Torsten

"Only a cryptic message to her remaining men, 'the time is now'," she says . "I did my part now will you allow me to visit my father?" she says.

"You can visit him after we return. I want you to deliver the message to her men and then I will watch them. They're sure to trip up and reveal where she is hiding this so called 'power' of hers," he says and the carriage leaves.

WARDEN"S QUARTERS BISMARCK PENITENTIARY

A call comes in from Seth Bullock to the warden N.F. Boucher.

"You have a visitor that our party wants you to extend

every courtesy towards within reason," he says.

"Yes, I know but I am not aware of her arrival. I made inquiries, she is not here -."

"Sir, you cannot be as inept as you sound. She is there, and you have vermin in your administration. See to both." Bullock hangs up the phone. The warden (N.F. Boucher) is beside himself. He is a prison reformer known for 'stretching' his authority.

Later in the day, the warden inquires if Madame Massey has arrived yet, and both the matron and officer Cromley deny knowing of her whereabouts. Bought and paid for is their ignorance. But, news of her presence spreads and within hours, Melvina has secured loyalty from many within the prison walls.

The culprits discovered, the warden now seeks other co-conspirators before showing his hand.

Meanwhile, back in Fargo, Anika does her part and alerts the men. Artemis thanks her and after she leaves, puts Melvina's plan into motion.

Telephone service in Fargo has existed since 1881. Three important men receive calls. The message is the same. "True power is not to dominate the weak, but to inspire the strong to do bold things. A lady needs you will you not help?"

Three days after her arrival, Melvina wakes from an afternoon nap to the loud rambunctious voice of an angry warden who has discovered the deceit within his prison. He apologizes to the mulatto Madame and escorts her to his new quarters where she stays for the rest of her term. No woman prisoner has resided in the warden's quarters. Before or after Melvina.

Torsten continues to watch the Crystal Palace; however, Artemis and Standing Bear are never seen coming or going, yet they end up in various places around the Hollow. Anika forgot to mention the clandestine tunnels.

The Color of Power

One night as Torsten is imbibing in one of the 100 bars in Moorhead, he goes to relieve himself. A moment into emptying his bladder, he feels metal on his throat and scrotum.

"Anytime, anywhere, this is how you will die. Remember this," he says. And then the knives are withdrawn. But not before drawing blood. Torsten is so shocked he does not turn his head to see who it was. Only one man in either town. Standing Bear, who is gone, on a wisp of air.

Home Again

Seven months later a train pulls into the Fargo depot and out of the car emerges Melvina Massey now known as the 'negress'. She enters the Crystal Palace where a grand party begins in her honor.

Melvina welcomes a young Amelia Marlowe and asks one question of her "So you want to be a whore?" The discussion does not go as the young woman imagines and she leaves with a different perspective of the sporting life.

"Child this is a bitter business in a bad world filled with bad people. You are not equipped to handle the business, the world, nor the people," Melvina says as she sips her tea. Amelia comes up with a witty retort but she knows better, and sits.

"You came here under the impression you knew what you wanted to do, but you will leave focused on the task I will set you on, or die, your choice," Melvina says and motions to someone off on the other side of the room.

Thora brings a small jewelry box made of pine with mother of pearl etchings to Madame Massey.

"I will send you on an adventure. Every young woman needs to have true-life experiences before settling down. Otherwise, you will settle for just any ole man and we cannot have that now can we?" the aging Madame says.

She opens the box filled with miscellaneous items from her many years and travels. There are diamond earrings, strings of pearls, silver necklaces inlaid with gemstones of various sorts. Melvina takes her time to explain the lot.

"Every woman needs jewelry because it is jewelry that sets her apart from every other woman. Now then, the diamond earrings are an accent piece; wear them when you first arrive in a new place. They give you a sense of station befitting a woman of your class. You wear the pearls and matching earrings on special occasions, a ball, or some other formal gathering. Again, they give a visual representation of your pedigree and most important, that you know when they are appropriate. The silver broach and necklaces garnished in gemstones are definitive attention grabbers. You will need to own at least two dresses with a 'décolletage' to not only display the gems, but an ample cleavage too," she says and continues as the young woman listens focused on every word.

"I have selected these two ornaments for you. They are less garish than some I have seen in these parts but each sends the message 'look at me, no not there, here,' and that is what we want to embody at all times young one," she coughs and sips more tea.

"Miss Massey, I mean Madam Massey I am honored and cannot wait to begin work I -."

"Shhhh child, you think you will work here...haha no chance in hell. I did not have a choice, well maybe I did. The sporting life is not a choice, but you have one. Why do you suppose I am investing time and precious money in you?" Melvina asks, and young Amelia flushed with embarrassment and bewilderment, chances a guess.

"I do not understand ma'am, I had assumed tha-."

"There you go again, white folks and their assumptions, presumptions and delusions. Child you are a woman in a fabulous time, the opportunity for you to prosper rests not in the hands of men, but in your ability to strike out and seize the moment. Frivolity and status quo are not for you, this is the time for young women to make their mark, to stand and be recognized as equal partners in this land. If they don't see us then by God they will hear us."

Melvina motions for Thora to step forward.

"This will be your companion and associate to St. Paul, where you will enroll in the University, and work as a secretary for the Minnesota Women's Suffrage Association. I have seen to your placements, and your grandfather will support your educational requirements," she says.

"He what, how did he -."

"Shhhh shhhhh I've been doing this for damn near forty years, how do you think I have prospered in a world of men that want to remain on top no matter how bad the circumstance? Your grandfather has always supported his children, your mother for example. Speaking of which, young Amelia, I dislike your mother, never have, never will like that woman. However, I respected her, admired her gumption and drive, but that was all a facade. She, like many women of the time, she defers to men and that has left her broken in more ways than one," she says as she stands and takes the young woman by her shoulders. "Listen I was a whore, and I managed whorehouses, but I never disrespected the women or men I employed. Whores own property, and are seen out on their own without men, yet our lives are in constant danger. So many of my sisters have died from abortions, opium or killing themselves. Amelia, this occupation is not for the weak. But damn what other choices did we have? I kept them healthy and safe, yet I can do no more. It is time for something else to emerge as the example of women's freedom and independence. So you go now with Thora. Do not look back to Fargo, there ain't nothing here but burnt offerings," she says and rejoins her party.

Amelia and Thora board the train in the morning with $300 dollars, and a pine box. They return to the area (Minnesota) at the death of Henry Massey, when they gather contributions to bury him.

My 'Shugga Bugga'

During the party, Melvina runs her fingers over the brim of a derby often worn by George Sands. A tear rolls down her cheek, Artemis hands her a glass of Champagne, still illegal to consume in Fargo, but no one will arrest her today, for the sheriff and two deputies are drinking.

"A toast to the fallen, the defiant, and the strong, may we all be as loyal in our walk of life as George Sands," she says, and the attendees say 'here here'. But her mind drifts back to that cold cell.

Melvina sits in the shadows, her mind enveloped with regret and the stench of her cell. She recalls a recent visit with her grandchildren, the 'Shugga Buggas' she called them.

Her only son Henry, had three children each more rambunctious and curious than the next.

Fred and Elva were always quick to impress their grandma with tales of Rhode Island life. However, grandma takes a liking to young Jane. Jane is always fascinated with the diamond earrings Melvina wore.

This fascination is the nickname her grandma gives her that will last an entire lifetime. 'Fascination' Massey, will also lead an extraordinary life. However, on this special trip to the Massey's of Rhode Island, Melvina comes bearing gifts and news.

She arrives in a carriage to the home of Henry and Anna Massey. Tired from the trip and feeling her 60years, the still beautiful woman enters the house to a rousing welcome.

"Now now yawl stop jumping on this old woman and where are my kisses?" she shouts at them. Loving every hug and kiss from these children. Melvina craved what Henry and Anna have, a house, children, community, and each other. But it was not the case for this Madame.

After dinner, she sits with Henry and Anna for some small talk, but in fact, it is a foreshadowing of things to come.

"How are your financials?" she says, and Henry is reticent to respond knowing his mother's intuition. She already has an answer. "I only ask because at some point you may be called to handle my affairs in Fargo. No telling how long that will take either, consider your options now, so that when the time comes you can act upon them," she says.

"Momma you will outlive us all I am sure," Anna says and excuses herself to check on the kids. Henry moves closer to his mother.

"What is wrong?" he asks.

"Henry, I have a terrible premonition of something terrible befalling us both. You need to hear me now, men dislike me for what I am and for what I know. But that knowledge is power, and I refuse to relinquish my grip on such a thing," she says.

"What do you know?" he asks.

"You're not cut from the same cloth to know my son. However, I have made accommodations if something were to befall me. My men have a code phrase that will set my retribution in motion," she says.

"Oh so clandestine and covert, tell me more," Henry says eager to hear his mother's mysterious machinations, fearing that they may just be figments of her imagination.

"The initial phrase will come from an untrustworthy source. That is how they know to move with all importance. They burn the evidence, make calls, and men of action take command. Once it begins there is no stopping it Henry," she sighs. "It is my best and only hand to play."

"Mother you speak in cryptic thoughts, power, and knowledge what does it all mean?"

he says.

"For many years I believed that white people held power because they were white. I fed their perceptions so I too could command power in whatever form. So misinformed was I, not until I met a man in Deadwood did I realize the color of power. It is knowledge, and knowledge can be any color, but for my purposes, I colored it green. Not as green as Fascination's eyes, no a mint green as in money. I parlayed my knowledge into money, to finance the Palace, and political alliances. Both of which will soon come to an end," she says.

Henry is still skeptical but continues to let his mother talk. To him it is all the grand delusions of a once beautiful woman now living out the rest of her life paranoid of men coming to take something from her. Henry does not understand, her knowledge, her power, her prosperity. He assumes she is as broke as he is, but then finds it hard to reconcile that with her ability to travel this great distance, and arrive bearing gifts. So he listens until she tires of talking and falls asleep.

He covers her with a wool blanket, and puts another log in the fireplace. As he turns to walk out of the room, he hears her say,

"Once I am gone they will come for everything, every last thing I own, do not let them break you."

He stops at the door and assures his mother,

"I won't, I am a Massey, and we are unbreakable," he

says and walks down the hall. Her eyes open to glimpse him for the last time. She makes out his silhouetted shape and a cold shiver runs up her spine. For the rest of her life, Melvina will feel cold whenever she thinks of Henry.

Madame Massey

The party ends and Melvina adjourns to her room. Contemplative is she and weary. Artemis and Standing Bear join her for their last tasks. They enter the room and are reluctant to address her; she senses this and begins the dialog.

"I have never been much for parties but this one warmed my heart. Please tell me our status in the houses and our arrangements in Moorhead," she asks. Artemis speaks first and reminds her of the issues over the last 7 months.

"Maam, it was a surprise to us when they killed George, rest in peace, but the Marlowe woman snapped us back into reality. She delivered the phrase -." Artemis says and Standing Bear interjects...

"As you had foretold, the bearer of this news is no friend. We changed our collection times, and used the tunnels more," he says.

"Yes my friend. The calls went out to the powerful in Chicago, St. Paul, and Bismarck. Within a day we could sense a difference," he says.

"How so Artemis, give me specifics," she asks.

"All the remaining madams are escorted out of town, and the court orders each boarding house closed and deemed 'not suitable for human inhabitants'," he says.

"Why that was heavy handed, but I suppose my benefactors wanted to make sure that the only pussy for sale in Fargo would be the pussy in my establishments. Considering how much they cost me to begin with, I would say that was an even exchange. How did the city council take it though?" she asks.

"You mean Torsten Marlowe; he took over a vacated seat and within a month was running the council. He did not like it one bit. No brothel revenue hinders most of the city services. By the third month, the threat of numerous strikes and walk offs made him resign his post. The new city manager, an appointee with our best interest at heart, opens more brothels in the Hollow," he says.

"You are hesitating, what is the catch?" she asks.

"We had to sell two properties so that other madams could come back. This was contingent upon your early release," he says and hands over the lease documents.

"These documents are for leasing the land and not selling it outright, I would have opted for the same. They pay me and the town, so this plan is working well is it not?" she asks, but both men do not seem as overjoyed as she is.

"The death of George is not something we bargained for regardless of the capital gains that will ensue. Your enemies are still many Madame Massey, and we are but a few," he says.

"You speak the truth Artemis, you always have, and that is why I want you both to take leave in the coming year. It is way past time you had wives and families of your own, before it is too late," she says. The men appreciate the show of charity but it is lost on them who are in their early 50s.

Melvina is not only thinking of them but her own mortality. Sometime over the last 7 months, regret has seeped into her life for the first time. Free, she can only provide hope to family and those she employs, and takes none for herself.

"We will have no more conversation on that topic,

however, I would like to know the state of our finances Artemis," she says with a smile full of daggers.

"Yes ma'am, just wanted to give you a full accounting, we have 15,000 dollars on hand," he says and Standing Bear laughs.

"Oh dear, times have been hard I see. We will proceed as if we have triple that. I want every room in the Crystal Palace decorated and contact Charlie Jones in Chicago. We will have a band here for Friday and Saturday evenings. Get it done Artemis, and Standing Bear..." she calls.

"Yes Miss Massey," he answers.

"Ensure that all the guests have departed and then I have a special task for you. Pack your bags, you will not be returning," she says. Standing Bear is to accompany Thora and Amelia to St. Paul. She gives him $500 for his expenses. He will never see Melvina again.

After the Party

1902-1907 FARGO

Melvina continues to thwart authorities who under-estimate her abilities. However, Torsten plays one final card. He bribes a few witnesses and a prosecutor. The prosecutor brings charges against Melvina once more for bootlegging. This time there is no doubt the face behind it all.

"This man, if I would have known how much of an irritant he would be, I would have never stopped screwing him," she says to her lawyer. "He is always overplaying his hand," she says.

"What did you do to him Melvina, and why is he so determined to see you rot in jail," he asks.

"I can only speculate that I refused to run off to San Francisco with him. He begged me frequently, saying he could embezzle his father-in-law's money to fund our expedition. Torsten enjoys living off the labor of others. He is such a pitiful excuse of a man."

The only day of the trial begins and ends with the first witness. A man 'who forgot his lines' and who says so in court. The judge dismisses the charges and Melvina winks at Torsten as he storms out of the courthouse.

She gives her lawyer a promissory note for his services. The note is for services rendered and against services in kind at the Crystal Palace.

"Fair exchange is no robbery dear one," she says as she passes him the note, which he accepts.

Months later, another man will take Melvina to court seeking recompense on the same note he received as payment for a service. He wants the dollar value but the judge sides with Melvina.

"This note is only good for the services one can get at the Palace. I would suggest that you try to redeem it with an amenable employee of said establishment. Case dismissed."

This is the last public appearance of the Mulatto Madame of Fargo. She arrived 20 years prior to seek a promised opportunity, fleeing from other promises not kept. Her life and times riddled with prosperity and treachery, yet she often found time to visit her loved ones in Rhode Island and Virginia.

Madame Massey remembers what her daddy told her so many years before.

"Perception is how they see us, and as sure as you're born, they always view us as less than them. So you decide, not them, you decide how they see you."

A Letter

On a crisp October morning in 1908, a letter arrives from
St. Paul. One of the last remaining Chinese residents of the
Crystal Palace, brings it to Madame Massey with her tea.
Melvina is wearing a shawl and is rocking near a window
that overlooks the street in front of the large home.

She takes her time opening the letter.

"Dear Madam Massey, I hope and pray this letter finds
you in good health and spirits. Thora and I have been ever
busy with the cause, and continue to bring more women
and men to this understanding. The purpose of this letter
is twofold: I want to reiterate my love and appreciation of
your great charity.

You have put me on a path I may never have come to
on my own, so I thank you once again. Second, I found
a compartment in the box and a list of 30 names and
addresses. At first I thought it was clients and then we
received your letter that stated

'There are things inside that will help you on your
journey. Use them with caution and only when obstacles
become overbearing'; and might I say that this list has
assisted us in every step of the way. We thank you and love
you Madam Massey, and we remain faithful to the power
you have shared. Yours Forever in sisterhood, Amelia"

Melvina tosses the letter into the fireplace. She stands
in front of her life-sized portrait and smiles. A sense of
calm and dread come over her as she realizes a singular
truth, her reality.

A familiar figure roams the halls of the Crystal Palace.
Artemis has returned from three years of travels in search
of his own fortune in Alaska, and a bride in Denver. He
is not successful in either. So he returns to his one true
home and the only woman he loves.

He enters the room as Melvina sits in a rocker facing

the street. Her trusted aid and dear friend Artemis is by her side. Theirs is a complex and intricate relationship. Formed out of a traumatic experience and forged over time, she respects him and he loves her. Yet there is always work that needs doing and when she requires his services, he never fails.

"What's wrong Melvina?" he asks as his hand touches her shoulder.

"They are coming for something I no longer have, power," she says.

Melvina reaches up to grasp the hand of her friend. She feels the comfort in his touch and something else, a Derringer.

"Then let them come," he says.

THE END

Massey Reunion

The Descendants

Melvina Massey (by accounts) lived an incredible life. Her thirst for life, independence, and knowledge, passes to her heirs. The following pages tie loose ends within the timeline and give you an idea of who these magnificent Massey men and women were.

There are outstanding questions the family historians had which form the bulk of our creative-fiction. The questions discuss gaps in the historical and chronological timelines and offer us a chance to speculate in many areas.

As mentioned earlier, the intent is to present the facts. We then add a pinch of speculation, to get you to either a reasonable doubt or an acceptance of a probability. In the case of probabilities, the goal is 85% or higher. Those numbers make sure a reader will seek more information, multiplying our eyes for research.

So how did I filter the facts from fiction and then decide on a probable (although speculative) course of action? It was not easy. However, reviewing the many notes of the family historians one night, I came across names used for over five generations. This tidbit of information helps to weave through so many possible Malvinas, Melvinas, Edwards, and Henrys scattered across northern Virginia and DC. This leads to an exchange between Massey family historians (3rd cousins Brandon and ShaRon) and a Debi Robison.

Her research identifies that the Carter family owns a slave girl named Mima. Mima was more than likely a concubine of either the owner or a son and has six mulatto children. The Carters keep her and the children together. They consider them 'family members'.

Now please understand the term mulatto means of mixed origin, specifically black and white. A mulatto slave is not necessarily 'light-skinned' but they are lighter than the African in bondage without race mixing.

The Carters consider both Mima and her children as family is a fact. It means the children have obvious European features (hair, eyes, and nose). This is a common practice within the Massey lineage. But not as common throughout the institution of slavery in America as a whole.

Ms. Robison's research data is interesting but what we found compelling is the information about a Margaret Ruffin. Melvina's obituary mentions Mrs. Ruffin but neither Brandon nor ShaRon could place her within the family. The Margaret Ruffin connection to Melvina (95% probability) from the new data shows a definitive family connection.

With that being said, lingering questions and doubts continue to surface even at this late stage of the print version, that need clarification.

Where was Melvina born and raised?

The question itself should not cause angst or anxiousness. But, in a time where Melvina and Malvina are common and interchangeable, the task was hard. Finding slaves birth records is a difficult task, but Melvina presents unique issues.

My observations, assessments, and speculation led me to the following statements.

1) The Carters owned a slave named Mima in the mid to late 1790s. She is more than likely a mulatto child who grows to become a cherished concubine of either her owner or another male heir.

2) Mima may have been acquired from a nearby slave-owner named Massey (this gets you the Massey DNA, and the Massey surname).

3) I surmise that this Massey needed to remove his daughter Mima, from his wife's sight. I cover why this was a common practice later. He sells her to his neighbors or relations, the Carters. So, we now have two generations of mulattos and one of Mima's sons, Edward, breeds with another mulatto on a nearby plantation. Their children (Melvina is one) are the third generation and have both Massey and Carter bloodlines. This is as close as I can come to a plausible explanation, but please continue reading.

There is a Massey surname but no Massey owners. Let us pause for just one second to let that sync. The only I can see a Massey in the DNA (of Henry Massey) is if Edward's slave wife was the child of a Massey and later sold.

However, Mima's children were calling themselves Massey by then, and the naming conventions typically relate to former masters whom the slaves (and their descendants) were close relations. Alternatively, could Mima herself be a Massey offspring? That could explain the Massey DNA (the Caucasian half of the family) and her children adopting the surname. However, this is speculation at best. The fact remains though, (if you subscribe to the proposed lineage) no Massey descendant of Mima, Edward, Melvina, Henry, was ever owned by a Massey to have Massey DNA. More on slave owners, concubines, and breeding information follows, as it plays an important part in this Massey story.

Thomas Jefferson decrees that the United States leave the international slave trade in 1808. This forces the slave owners to increase their stocks through breeding instead of imports. The total number of slaves in America at the time is 1,192,362, or 20% of the population (according to the 1810 census).

Breeding of slaves will increase this number to 6 million by 1865. Another unintended consequence is the high number of 'mulattoes' in the general population (1830 census). By Melvina's, birth (1835-1838) census takers classify Americans as either White, Black, or Mulatto.

How did another ethnic group evolve? During this same period, the international demand for cotton becomes the catalyst of the industrial revolution. The need to increase slave stock becomes crucial for the planters, especially those cotton farms supplying this raw material. Planters grow cotton, tobacco, and now slaves. Before we discuss this topic, let us explore facts on the sexploitation of slaves, when Melvina (1838-1865) is a slave.

Female slaves (males as well) were subjects of brutal and inhumane treatment and sexual abuse throughout the institution of slavery and into the next century. Slave women had no authority over their bodies nor the offspring they produce. The master controls whom she has sex with and marries. In addition, slavers try to pair slaves that fancy each other, or they go to great lengths to pair logical mates based on physical attributes consistent with the slave they wish to produce strong, healthy laborers.

RACE MIXING AND COHABITATION

It was common for a master to take the prettiest of his slave girls as concubines drawing the ire and wrath of his wife but not always. Most slave owner's wives understand that any fruit from these illicit and immoral liaisons are a valuable commodity just as any other slave. So, they were on board for that reason alone.

There are countless tales and accounts of wives taking different vindictive and bloody paths. The concubines know to avoid the master's wife when the master is away else suffer at her hands. This terror spreads to the infants, as many become the victims of beheading or strangulation in their cribs. Planters often sell the concubine and her baby to appease their wives.

The infants most likely to escape such atrocities are

often the offspring of a son or brother, cohabitating with a slave, and the child possesses European features. The prevailing thought for decades was that privileges were extended to these children. Mulatto babies did not enjoy as much liberty, and stood more chance of auction or death, than others.

So making sure you are tracking this right, in 1808, the import of slaves from Africa is illegal, so planters breed slaves to support the growing cotton crop. These same planters (some not everyone, but enough), raped slaves and cohabitated with them in parts of the country. This practice drew extreme disgust from northern abolitionists who viewed this as an abomination. To own a human being and cohabitate with them is immoral, hypocritical, and inhumane. This practice creates incestuous relations in the master's house, between his mulatto slaves and his own children.

The raping of slave women is not limited to the master and his son. Any slave woman, especially a light skinned or mulatto is always in danger of a stalker who will, pursue, and eventually rape her. White men working on the plantation use this practice to keep their captives in fear.

BIRTH AND PATERNITY

Melvina's son, Henry James Massey (born a slave) but we could not find the year or his father. One record of slave births in Loudon County Virginia for April 18, 1858, shows a boy named 'James H' (no last name) born to a woman (slave) named Melvina, at the Ross residence. There is no mention of the father.

The same 1870 census that does not list Henry living with his father, does not show Melvina either. This has led us to speculate that maybe from 1867-1875 she was somewhere else. Possibly, refining her skills in the sex trade, or could she have been in this business longer than we think? Truth is we cannot say one way or the other but we know she visited Henry and his family many times. Was this guilt on her part? Did Henry welcome these excursions? These are questions we may never have answers for, but everything in Henry's life is the opposite of Melvina's. That alone is compelling.

DID MELVINA HAVE MORE CHILDREN?

From Melvina's timeline, we know a George Cuthbert Powell sells her at 13, to a John F. Ross. She is at perfect breeding age to begin. We assume that with her being a light mulatto girl that her owner kept her close as a concubine or breeder. Remember the idea is to increase your stock. Given her age, the master expects Melvina to have three to four children by 20.

We can find no evidence of other children besides Henry, but, on her booking documents in Bismarck (1900) she says she has 'two other children in DC but do not know if they are dead or alive.' If this statement is true (Melvina often pushed the bounds of truth), were these children fathered by a Ross or Gray and sold?

Now given the lascivious nature of slave masters (and their breeding practices), the next leap is that Melvina bore two children before turning 20 (when Henry is born). What happens to these children?

Well, John Ross is married. It is possible that his wife directs him to sell his own children. However, another possibility follows. The Powell estate auctions off Melvina to a John H. Simpson in 1849. There is no record of Simpson selling Melvina to John Ross but we know he is in possession of a slave named Melvina before 1860.

Sometime between 1849 and 1858, Melvina has two children and Ross acquires her. Simpson has major debt issues and leaves Fairfax County for Texas in 1862, taking his slaves with him.

The speculation that she had other children follows

the practice of the day (breeding young women) and her own words at booking 'I don't know if they are alive or dead'. Her two children could have been five or six years of age when Ross acquires her. Simpson moves to Texas and takes his slaves.

WHO WAS HENRY'S FATHER?

Two other possibilities exist for Henry's father.

First, if Melvina was the concubine of John F. Ross, and his wife made him sell off two of his children (before age 20), suppose (to appease his wife's concerns) he acquires a suitable husband for Melvina. This male comes from the Gray farm/plantation, (a normal practice) and is mulatto as well (his mother was either a concubine, or his father a product of such a coupling with a Gray).

The couple is together until Melvina has a son right before the Civil War. This makes sense but, Henry's father is not with him in 1870, and likely that he never was with the boy throughout the war years.

This is loose conjecture but, the DNA from Massey's in Rhode Island, trace back to a Joseph Glass Gray, brother of William H. Gray, husband of Ellen D. Powell, cousin of George Cuthbert Powell Melvina's original owner.

Secondly, let us suppose once again that Melvina is indeed a concubine, and the other factors are true (birthed two children that were later sold). Ross swears not to frequent Melvina's cabin, but does offer access to his neighbors, the Grays. Once again, Melvina is pregnant, and the wife is livid. Ross is not the father (a Gray or a blood relation is) but she will hear none of it until Melvina and the child are both gone.

Secession and Civil War loom large in many minds at this time (1858-1860). If Ross decides to sell Melvina and Henry, he stands to gain a lot of money. However, no evidence of a sale exists, and Melvina never on the 'Freedman' list for northern Va or DC. So, the thought is that she is part of a trade (goods and services) or given away (a valuable gift). But to who?

The logical guess is that she goes back to the Powell's, or is allowed to stay on the Gray farm with her slave-law husband. Given the proximity of the farms/plantations, and the fact that the Grays are related to the Powell's this makes sense. So let us follow along this path.

Ross gives (barters?) both Melvina and Henry to his neighbors the Grays. They in turn pass them back to the Powell family, or (because of the relations), she is able to travel freely from both plantations. This brings Melvina and Henry back to Edward where she stays until 1863 (emancipation) or when the war is over in 1865.

DNA traces the Massey descendants to blood relatives of the Gray family and not the Ross. This supports both theories; but, we believe a Gray (part black or not) and Melvina had relations that produce Henry. The absence of a father either in birth records or in the 1870 census is telling. Was he dead, did he know he was a father? On the other hand, was the real father a wealthy southern man, who fathered children outside of his marriage that he never claimed? The latter fits the profile of discarded children and it sets the stage for another question.

WHAT WERE THE NAMING CONVENTIONS USED?

Did Henry and Anna Massey, leave ancestry bread-crumbs in the way they named their children? Their children and grand kids have similar naming conventions. First names are from Massey, Howard, and Coyle (planters/owners although we can find no Massey owners) lines.

However, they then use the surnames as middle names for Gray, Howard, and Coyle. Carter, Ross, and Powell do not appear in this manner. Was this an intentional way to pay homage to their masters who treated them grand or a way to ensure any perceived rights as heirs?

This practice stops after the third generation of Henry

and Anna descendants. Anna and her brother both benefit from being grandchildren of a former slave owner. They were deeded lands as caretakers, or outright. Lands Anna later sells for a pittance.

WHERE ARE THE MASSEY SLAVE OWNERS?

As mentioned, the line of descendants from Mima, to Henry, shows no trace of a Massey owner or DNA relations. If you disregard the entire Mima story, you still have Edward (owned by the Powell's), and Melvina (owned by Powell, Simpson, and Ross) but no Massey to where they adopt the surname.

Edward is using the Massey surname when he begins to have children with Caroline.

So you cannot disregard the Mima evidence for two reasons:

1. Mima may be where the Massey line begins, as we cannot discern whether she was an imported slave from Africa, or a mulatto child raised in a home (Massey) and then sold to the Carters.
2. The latter is more probable given that her children adopt the Massey surname, but they are products of Carters, not Massey. We have established a common naming convention among this family was to adopt the surnames of benevolent owners that took them in as part of the family. So given this information, why is Carter not their adopted surname?

The answer lies with Mima herself who was a valuable piece of the Massey family before auction. Speculations but consider what we know of this family's lineage up through 1900s. Four consecutive generations of mulattos with Mima at the head, naming conventions, and no possible owner to offer Massey DNA before Edward (other than Mima), points to Mima.

BOOTLEGGING

Was the burning of the Crystal Palace (in 1891) arson and is this arson related to Melvina's bootlegging? The bootlegging conviction in 1900 ends a decade on the run for Melvina. From the time she purchases the property and builds the Crystal Palace, Melvina is constantly harassed and possibly extorted. But why her and why now?

When researching the historical facts associated with her life in Fargo, this period stood out as both intriguing and counter-intuitive. The 'Mulatto Madame' lives in comfort. She dines at the best restaurants and establishments in Fargo and Moorehead. Melvina builds the grand Crystal Palace, and rebuilds it immediately after the fire.

Madame Massey is rich and influential. Yet despite her status, the county prosecutor pursues her at every opportunity. This lasts for over a decade.

They wanted her and the state's own record on prosecuting bootleggers' bears this out. Melvina is the last person to serve a sentence for bootlegging in North Dakota. There were only two.

So why Melvina Massey, what did she do to deserve such infamous notoriety? Was her ethnicity the root?

MELVINA'S ETHNICITY IS IN QUESTION

The region's historians split over this often stating that the people of Fargo 'knew' implying that her physical features were that of a colored or black person. Folks even support the claim by saying 'I've seen a picture' yet we have found no pictures of Melvina, to include her photo taken at booking.

Newspaper accounts of brothel raids in Fargo and Minnesota in the 1880-90s, mention madams and Madam Massey (specifically) but never her ethnicity. The assumption is that these madams are white. Otherwise, the articles would distinguish between them by stating colored, black, or Negress. Her race comes into question during and after her trials (1898-1901).

Even reports of the Crystal Palace being a 'Coon dive' (term used by white men seeking black prostitutes) never attributes the owner as being nothing other than a madam.

They say the circumstantial evidence is 'inconclusive'. What we say is that Melvina Massey is a third generation mulatto; and on June 6 1900, a census investigator annotates that Melvina Rae (she marries Charles AKA Henry Rae in 1893) is 'white' and a widower.

Yet miraculously one year later, in an article on her sentencing, the Jamestown Weekly Alert refers to Melvina as a 'disreputable colored person'. However, rhetorically asks what might have been the sentence if it were 'a more prominent (prominent equates to white) person that committed the crime'. One can only speculate that from 1898-1901, the facade of Melvina's 'whiteness' erodes and now she is known as 'the negress' hereafter.

HOW WEALTHY WAS SHE?

Her wealth is in dispute. Melvina amasses a fortune and lives a grand life. But, not for long. There can be no doubt on what her final estate was in 1911 (valued at around 1,000, 30k in today's money). However, given the time between her death and her son's arrival in Fargo, you have to believe a few of her belongings 'grew legs' and walked out of the Crystal Palace.

When determining the accuracy of her wealth two important factors are in play here, one is her ability to rebuild her grand palace shortly after the arson. Now either she has a knack for saving money or an inexhaustible pipeline of funding.

The money, always follow the money. A person with this liquidity shortly after a fire during the worst depression ever (1893) must have access to money whenever she needs it. Fact 2 is the likelihood that her funds come from bootlegging not prostitution.

Another interesting fact is Melvina leaving Fargo after her brothel closes in 1899-1900. She hides out in 'Old Portage' aka 'Rat Portage' aka Kenora. This lucrative mining region is a haunt for smugglers and bootleggers before prohibition.

So why is this important? The twin city of Moorehead has over 400 bars and pubs during this time and one has to wonder who supplies them?

Suppose that the key to Melvina's disposable income is not her brothel (s) but her ability to supply smuggled alcohol into Moorehead and other parts of Minnesota, avoiding the alcohol tax. She sells this booze at wholesale undercutting the legitimate distributors. This enterprise makes Melvina very wealthy and an enemy to those trying to sell above board.

Critics will call this conjecture. However, when you line the facts up they point to a successful bootlegger. Melvina ran a brothel, but it is not why the law pursues her for a decade.

MELVINA ON TRIAL

Now given that, she is on probation from an earlier issue with selling alcohol (they never show whether she was distributing the prohibited item, or just selling it in her establishment). This infraction usually garners no more than a fine and probation. The second offense is interesting given the overzealous prosecutor in his pursuits of Madame Massey.

Eyewitnesses report that Melvina sells alcohol in the Crystal Palace. The trial suffers delays because the 'witnesses' are missing. Two years later, a judge dismisses similar claims, from another witness because the man forgot his 'lines'. This is a curious fact that throws shade on her earlier indictments and trials. Had Clay County prosecutors trumped up charges and suborned perjury? In light of the evidence, one might lean towards such an assumption. But, why Melvina Massey?

The answer is obvious yet subtle, given what we have from history; Melvina Massey was a very successful bootlegger. Her understanding of how to circumvent prohibition enforcement in North Dakota and her ability to supply thirsty drinkers in each of the bordering states is visionary. No one else will put the two together until forty years later during the prohibition era.

Her lucrative endeavor brought her under heavy scrutiny from both sides of the law. Intimidation comes when the Crystal Palace burns to the ground. By 1899-1900, with her brothel closed, she retreats to the lucrative mining region of Rat Portage for a time to check on her supply chain and other business opportunities.

This is speculation but one cannot possibly believe a woman of her intelligence opens herself up to scrutiny and prosecution by selling a few drinks in the Crystal Palace. Not when she is supplying hundreds of bars in Moorehead, this is the dilemma in trying to unravel Melvina's life. Once you believe you have isolated the facts, up comes something new to cast doubt upon the entire thing.

Her 'holding out' in Rat Portage is an example of this, for in one hand, we have a significant find, which underscores a possible smuggling connection. Without this information, it was hard to understand why Cass County prosecutors are so aggressive in their pursuit of a lowly Madame serving alcohol in a suspected 'bawdy house' that they fabricated charges and witnesses. Melvina Massey is always more than what you see.

May be their aggressiveness is just a sign of the times, with prohibition and evangelism sweeping through the territory, chasing and purging the town of whores and booze makes perfect sense. Yet we know the Crystal Palace operated on and off from 1891-1911, so just how aggressive were they?

In summary, we find ourselves once again asking questions that defy logic (given this Nation's history) and the facts history provides. Are we to believe this fourth generation mulatto arrives in Fargo and receives every privilege befitting a white madam? Or did the towns people know she was black the entire time and let her conduct business like everyone else? Was she an infamous Madame, bootlegger, or both? Of all the madams and bootleggers in Cass County, why did they come after Melvina Massey so aggressively?

It boils down to the authorities in Cass County dedicated to enforcing the state's prohibition laws. Especially against a mulatto Madame, whom they once believed was white.

THE DESCENDANTS

In closing, this section of the book comprises speculative and creative historical fiction. I am endeavoring to piece to together three components; Henry Massey from birth to Rhode Island; the last days of Melvina, and Fascination and her husband Abraham.

Once again, I will fill in the gaps that history left out, with speculation and best guesses. Each of which belies the nature of the Massey legacy in general, they lived, they prospered, and the rest is a mystery.

Conjugal Visits

A large carriage leaves the Loudon County courthouse following close behind is buckboard with five recently purchased slaves. The year is 1849, and James H. Simpson is leaving an estate auction for the deceased George Cuthbert Powell of Loudon County. They make their way on the road in constant lookout for highwaymen known to prowl in the county.

Overseer Thaddeus McPhee pulls alongside of the lead carriage. His face carries distress among its many wrinkles.

"Boss I do not want to alarm you but a small pack of men is following us,"

"Ever the one for the dramatic huh Thaddeus?" Simpson slows the carriage. "How many and for how long?"

"Two since the courthouse and seven more for the last eight miles, give or take,"

"That's nine to our five. Advise me when we approach the 15 mile marker, the farm and friends will be close then,"

"But sir that's another six miles, do we want to risk the merchandise for folly?" McPhee startles Simpson who is not afraid of any man or beast.

"Thaddeus now you have me worried whereas before I was somewhat concerned, but now my curiosity is piqued because you seem agitated. I do not want my overseer agitated on this 20 mile excursion, so in the parlance of a nickel whore waiting for her next John, out with it man," McPhee wastes little time in relaying his thoughts on the rogues chasing them.

"These are scoundrels' boss. They size up the wealthy landowner returning from an auction and rob him of his merchandise and valuables. Then they whisk the human cargo to Tennessee for auctions in Mississippi, Orleans, and Arkansas,"

"I see, with the need for slaves in the deep south at all-time highs you are right to urge caution. Those planters in the south run their slaves ragged and then wonder why their birth rates are so low,"

"So what's our play sir?"

"The element of surprise is with them; however we need to know what we don't know first Thaddeus. There are two men trailing us, which we outnumber. You count an additional seven more which have gone ahead looking for a suitable ambush point," Simpson assesses his odds and decides to run to fight. "You send two men up ahead to scout out access to the road from the north. There is another road a mile from this approaching bluff. We take it and then high tail it as fast as possible into Fauquier County. They want to test us further out away from any help. Well we will not oblige them today," Simpson kicks his horses into a faster trot and McPhee organizes the men.

The slaves riding in the buckboard, Peyton, Lavinia, Washington, Melvina, and Charles, look on in wonderment as the white folks scurry. Charles is only six and has a bevy of questions for Melvina, who tells him to be quiet and hope they die.

Simpson and party round the bend and speed up the alternate path which will take them five miles out of their way. But, they will arrive safe. His two men return with good news and bad news. The good news is they saw men ahead; the bad news is there are ten of them.

For all of his smarts in outwitting them, Simpson knows he is still out-gunned. So, he comes up with another plan. He sends one man with the rest of his cash on ahead for the sheriff. He then stops and makes camp.

"Sir beg pardon, but why are we sitting here waiting

for the inevitable?"

"The men following us despite our shenanigans will be here within an hour, the rest two maybe three. Hixon who we sent for the sheriff -."

"One and a half, the Sheriff will arrive before they have us out-gunned, so what then?"

"Well I say the two in hot pursuit will be in need of a drink, a poke, and cash,"

"Sounds right boss, you suppose you gonna give them that young one?"

"Oh no she is choice breeding stock and will always fetch a good penny for domestic bed warming services and so on,"

"I like how you think sir," McPhee turns and gives orders to the remaining men. They remove the slaves from the buckboard and tie them to it. Except Lavinia, in her late 20s, dark even toned skin, with an ample bosom and tight hips. The men remove her top exposing her breasts. Melvina puts her hands over Charles's eyes.

Within an hour two riders approach and sure enough they agree to the barter without hesitance. McPhee has a notion to put a bullet in them. But waits for the Sheriff.

"Look at them McPhee,"

"Must I boss?"

"Look at the takers of our society and how craven they are," the men ravage Lavinia for a turn each and one goes for seconds against her protest. Melvina continues to shield the young boy from the sights but the sounds are just as haunting. Simpson looks at his watch and then at McPhee. "On second thought I changed my mind. Lynch these fools."

McPhee and the other four men raise their weapons and with one shot fell a highwayman. The other man scampers to put his britches on. He pleas for his life in vain.

"We had a deal."

"Who parlays with the likes of you? Especially after, you have defiled my property. Mr. McPhee, hang this one, shooting is too damn good for him," McPhee wastes no time and hangs the man in front of the slaves.

The Sheriff arrives 30 minutes before the remaining crew, which hightails it into the backwoods. Two are dead, and three captured. Simpson explains his reasons for administering vigilante justice to his cousin the Sheriff who allows him to go ahead on home.

TWO YEARS LATER SIMPSON FARM

Melvina is now 15 and gives birth to one child a boy from a coupling with an aggressive buck that will not take no for an answer. After the birth, Simpson tries to pair her with different men with the same result she spurns every last one.

He does not give up though and brings in another older male. The man is big, brawny, and hideous. But, he is a powerful worker, and that's what Simpson is most keyed upon is prime breeding stock. Jeremiah arrives in Melvina's cabin with her and the child. She knows what is going to happen and she will have no part of it.

The overseer locks them in for the night and laughs as he walks away. Melvina is polite at first thinking it's the best way forward. However, within an hour she knows he is here for one thing only. She walks over to the hearth, and he grabs her from behind, she pleads to put the baby asleep first. The older Jeremiah eases back.

Melvina lunges for the poker and her carving knife and stands between the baby and Jeremiah, now looming over her.

"I gots no problem with you mister and I know you just here to do masters bidding. But not with me, and not tonight," She balances herself ready to die than to be another victim on this plantation. "They took me once and that night I swore no man will ever have me unless I gave it to him on my own,"

"Child put the poker and knife away, master will have us do what he say do and nothing less," he tries to reason with the mad woman who looks white.

"Mister I aint gonna tell you again,"

"Child please I aint no mister it's Jeremiah. Call me Jeremiah," he tries to bring her emotions to a low boil but not Melvina.

"You're here to make something that master can sell. That is all they gonna do with these children is sell them at auction to another farm or plantation. Take them away from their kin, their friends. It's a lonely place out there Jeremiah I know, I know too damn well," her arm wavers from holding the poker. Melvina is no field hand so strength is not one of her strong suits, but her mind is quick and that is what will always save her.

"You may be right -."

"Maybe, nigger please, you old enough to know better Jeremiah. They just gonna sell these babies as fast as I can get them to walking and talking. I don't wanna do this again no I cannot,"

A few moments pass by and he tries to move towards her once more.

"What I say nigger? One more step and you either get'n poked with this hot iron or stabbed with the knife. Your choice," Jeremiah eases back and sits in the only chair her cabin has. This is the standoff.

TWO HOURS LATER

Melvina sits against the wall with her blouse opened. Jeremiah is sitting in the chair rocking her baby. She doesn't know what happened.

"The thing about you hi-yella heffas is that you rarely ever get out into the fields. You're always in the house or near to it. Yup, you pretty ones the masters keep an eye on. They have their reasons and I can't say as I blame them. You got tired from holding that poker up and fainted. I fed the baby. He will sleep through the night now. You should feed him more Melvina that boy latched on to your teat as if it was a gold nugget. Hahaha,"

"Why thank you kindly Mr. Jeremiah. I feel so awful for treating you this way. I am sorry," holding out her arms to take the child. Jeremiah gives him up and Melvina lies on her bed with the little boy. She falls off for a while with the child still nursing, then her eyes open wide and scan the room. Jeremiah is not here.

'Maybe they came and let him out while I was asleep, but I didn't hear a sound,' she thinks. Her body relaxes and then she feels it. Melvina has a terrible feeling that someone is in her bed behind her and waiting to pounce. A big thick hand the size of her head grabs her from the back of the neck. He has her entire neck in his palm and he squeezes.

"Master will have what is his. He sent me in here to do a job and no hi-yella youngin is gonna stop me. This how we gonna lay and I will take you until I can't no more,"

"Jeremiah you don't -." She could not get the words out quick enough for the big man to have lifted her dress and garments. He was doing what he came to do. Melvina stares at the fireplace. It's warming glow. In the flickers of those flames, she makes a promise.

"Every man will pay from now on, every last one."

THREE YEARS LATER

Simpson, with mounting gambling debts, sells off both Melvina's two sons and further bad investments force him to sell off more slaves. He sells Melvina to a John Ross where she becomes a domestic, often loaned out to clean a bordello 10 miles from his farm. She does similar work for Dr. Joseph Glass Gray before 1858.

Henry Massey 1858-1916 Arrives in Fargo to settle his mother's estate. Spends the rest of his life in court battles over her property.

When Henry met Anna

RICHMOND VIRGINIA CHRISTMAS EVE 1879

In a small alcove away from the main body of people, Henry and his mother Melvina have one last word on his pending nuptials. He tries to calm her, she is not a willing participant.

"Henry Gray -."

"Mother must you always put that name in my face?" He asks with a smile for the onlookers but his words are not friendly.

"I will do what I bloody damn well please, Henry Gray. You recognize that lineage for what it is not what it was. Ya never know where your life will lead and you may need to lean on your 'white folk' to assist," looking about the 2nd Baptist church.

"Those folk had nothing to do with me then so why expect a change?" He reaches to his mother and grasps her hands. "Tell me what is troubling you?"

"I don't trust her fast ass," Melvina's eyes glance over at the Pastor Scott. "Her or that pretentious father, mark my words, he is marrying her off in a hurry for a reason."

"Mother your mouth, remember where we are, and why do you say such things?"

"Henry, my sweet boy, this woman loves adoration, and she continues to welcome her previous lovers into her bosom. Charlotte is a sporting woman of another kind, the type that craves attention from men in droves. Not for sex, but to fill a void only attention can fill."

"Mother you have only met her once. How could you possibly assume -."

"Boy please, I know hoes, it's my business to know hoes," Henry agrees with his mother on that topic.

"Yes mother you do know whores and pimps."

"Yes I do."

"So what would you, oh Madame Massey, have me do?" Henry's sardonic question elicits a menacing look from his mother.

"Boy do not test me today, not today," she pauses for a second and grips Henry's hands tighter. "The first time I met your betrothed was two months ago. She did not know who I was at the time because I arrived fashionably late and mingled within the crowd. Young Charlotte stood five feet from me, entertaining various men vying for her attention. I wondered where you were during this time, and then I notice two men becoming 'comfortable' in their mannerisms and vocabulary around young Charlotte. It was a comfort one affords a lover or a familiar customer," Melvina's luxurious eyes capture Henry, and she looks deep in his soul. "Watch that hussy, for she is the worst kind of sporting woman. She does it for free."

The sound of the church organ breaks Melvina's hold on Henry and the two take their places as the ceremony begins. Her words ring in Henry's mind never leaving, for she plants the seeds of doubt in a fertile field. Alonzo Massey walks forward and motions for Henry to take his place. He offers his arm to Melvina.

"Alonzo, where are you leading me to now?"

"Well it aint to that fancy place in Chicago we went to that's for sure," the two share a small moment before Melvina asks him a question.

"Cousin, do you think he will be-."

"Who, Henry, he's fine. I will look after him not to worry."

"That's what worries me the most. You Massey men, I swear." The two have another laugh before she reaches her seat at the pew.

FALLS CHURCH VA 1880

Henry and Charlotte live with his grandfather, Edward Massey, his wife Lucy, and their grandson Arthur Blue (a mulatto age six). It has been a year since their first-born dies. They share the home with a 25-year-old black man, Reggie Webster and Edward's (adopted) son John Bell (age 15).

This is a cozy home fraught with possible 'awkward' situations given Charlotte's nature to be friendly with the males. Lucy speaks to her on many occasions on her attire and closing the door when changing. Which she disregards choosing to use a wardrobe screen for cover. Reggie and John suspect where her promiscuous attentions are leading. She throws an occasional flirt towards Edward too.

It is early on a lazy Saturday when Edward and Henry head out into the tobacco fields. Once they reach the fields a quarter-mile from the house, Henry realizes he has left something and heads back.

"What you forget?" Edward keeps working.

"My sweat rag, I usually carry two with me, but have not brought either,"

"Hmmm ya only need one, and I have another for you right here," he offers a dingy old rag.

"No thank you, grandpa, I will run back and get my own." Edward looks at the rag and his grandson.

"What is my rag not good enough for you Mr. high and mighty?"

"No grandpa, but it is too grimy for me," laughing at the gesture. "I will fetch the others."

"Make sure you do just that," Henry hurries back to the four-room house. He sees Lucy tossing out leftovers for the pigs. She looks at him and shakes her head. Henry sees Lucy talking to herself. She is often in her own state of mind on most days. Still, he moves towards the back of the house where the laundry hangs, in a cautious manner.

There among the clothes and linen, he hunts for a few rags when he hears his wife laughing. The laughter is peculiar to him. Playful giggles and something alluring. He smiles wondering if Charlotte is playing with the dog, but as he makes his way past the clotheslines, he does not see her. The laughter is coming from inside the house.

Henry steps on a stool and looks through a window to see his wife scampering around the room in just an undergarment, laughing. She is chasing young John around the room. He has a towel in one hand and her dress. Henry laughs himself harmless fun between in-laws. He notices someone else in the room. Reggie runs behind Charlotte and grabs her. This too is innocent enough except Henry senses more than play.

Reggie's hips are gyrating and his hands grope his wife in ways only meant for him, her husband. She laughs and does not scold Reggie. Charlotte turns to kiss him on the mouth, which only makes him take bolder liberties. Young John turns red in the face and backs out of the room.

"Now Reggie you need to stop before your desires take over your mind," she cautions while welcoming every naughty touch.

"My passion is burning hot, and it's your fault, putting it in my face every day," lost in their own lust they do not notice other voices in the front room.

"John, you and Reggie get to the fields right now. We have a full day ahead of us and you will pull your share today," Henry shouts and storms off back to the fields.

"Oh my God its Henry, you think he saw or heard us?" Charlotte tries to extract herself from Reggie's lustful grasp.

"Who cares, you rose my nature, and I need you to take care of it."

"Get off me, Reggie. Now is not the time. I wonder if he knows?" Charlotte pushes Reggie to the side and when he attempts to re-engage the naughty embrace, she punches him in his groin. "I said stop. You keep this up and I won't ever let you touch me again. Ya hear me Reggie?" he nods and saunters off to the front room where John awaits. They leave the house and follow a good twenty yards behind Henry.

Henry makes it back to Edward and is quiet and focused the rest of the morning. Edward looks back at the house and then Henry throughout the day. He suspects something occurred earlier to disturb his grandson, so he takes the opportunity during a short lunch break to speak his mind.

"Ya know we have family up in Rhode Island that I have been meaning to contact for a while. They say it is comfortable up there. But the winters are not hospitable," he lets the thought stick in the air for a moment. Henry chomps on the biscuits and tea Lucy brought out to them. An awkward moment between them is broken.

"What can't you say, Grandpa? That I am a fool?"

"No son, not at all. I say we have family in Rhode Island that will love to see Henry Massey for a short spell," he offers his grandson his last biscuit. "I'm saying that your type of marriage often needs time apart from each other before words are said in haste."

Henry takes the biscuit and chews hard.

"I understand, but haste or not, these words got to be said, and I aim to say all I need as soon as we are finished," the older Massey nods. "Oh and grandpa, write those relatives. I leave in the morning."

1881 FALLS CHURCH VA

Henry returns to Falls Church to attend a spring picnic at the Alfred St. Church. Alonzo Massey and Henry's wife Charlotte are present. Someone here will steal Henry's, heart.

Her name is Anna Jackson and her brother Franklin

(Frank or Freddie for short) accompanies her. Both of the Jackson's are mulattos but (due to their physical features) could easily pass for white in most anywhere in the country. They are visiting family but have been living in Rhode Island for four to five years now.

Henry met both of them previously but draws a blank when Alonzo introduces the couple once more.

"Freddie and Anna, this is my younger cousin Henry Massey," a distracted Henry nods at the couple. Anna takes notice of this and proceeds to scold him.

"See Freddie, a woman distracts him once again," Henry looks over at his promiscuous wife and the men adoring her. "This is the second time in a year we have met without so much as a 'please to make your acquaintance' from him," her grin is taunting. Henry snaps out of his distraction when Alonzo elbows him in the ribs. He turns to Alonzo frustrated and annoyed, only to fall victim to love.

"This is the young lady I was referring to back at the house," Alonzo motions to Henry. "Please excuse my young cousin; he is trying to locate his wife... again,"

"Wives should never be a distraction in public, well at least not for their husbands," Anna throws another open invite to Henry who focuses on her attire and grace. Anna wears a fashionable peach dress befitting the season, but her attire is not what ensnares him. She is of mixed breeding, another mulatto but she is much lighter.

If he did not know of her ethnicity, he would wonder why his cousin introduced him to a white woman in the first place. Her brother Freddie is often mistaken for a white man, and he leverages that at every opportunity, especially in the south.

Henry cannot escape Anna's eyes, and in this moment time freezes. Anna captures Henry with her wit and a splendid aura of good will surrounding her. He cannot remove his eyes from her gaze. His deep focus becomes embarrassing to Anna who begins to blush.

"Has Mr. Massey found a new distraction?" Laughter and cackling disrupt this pleasant romantic interlude. Two men vie for Charlotte's attention and her husband notices.

Henry takes Anna's hand into his, and kisses the back, "Miss Jackson, it is an honor to make your acquaintance," his eyes never break from her gaze.

Anna's heart thumps so loud within her chest that she looks to see if others hear it too.

"Well you met me too; do I get a kiss as well?" Freddie's small joke lightens the otherwise tense and awkward moment.

"Pleased to meet you, Freddie, now if you both will excuse me, I need to address something," Henry bows and turns to walk away. Alonzo joins him. They march to Charlotte.

"I know these two men. Let me escort them away from you two,"

"Be quick Alonzo, I have words for my wife,"

"Mind yourself, Henry. That's a wife you left here alone for over eight months," he politely escorts the other men to cold beverages.

Henry walks up to Charlotte, who is under the influence of either alcohol or a narcotic. Then again, Charlotte's eyes are always wild in nature.

"Enjoying yourself... wife?" her eyes widen in response.

"You say that like it still means something... to you," she turns her head to see the crowd.

"Such a brazen display, I can only imagine how you behave in private, you should at least act the part in public Charlotte,"

"What do you care Henry Massey? You abandoned me while you ventured off up north," with a slight tone of indignation.

"You are my wife and I-." She holds up her hand.

"Don't you dare say what you know is false. Your mouth may claim me but your heart is frigid Henry," her words confuse him for a moment. Henry is at a fork in the road where he must finally decide on whether to invest whole-heartedly in his marriage or give up. But, he chooses to lie instead.

"Of course I love you, Charlotte, why else would I come back?"

"Oh I don't know Henry, why did you leave in the first place?" Henry gives her a stern look as he grits his teeth before answering.

"You know good and damn well why I left. You are evil and your promiscuous ways, embarrassed me in front of my kin. You always had contempt for this marriage Charlotte, as if it was a prison,"

"That was all fun honey. If I wanted to give out pokes you think I could stop 'your kin' in that small house?"

"Watch your tongue harlot!"

"Harlot, no that's your momma -." Henry grabs Charlotte by the upper arms and pulls her to within an inch of his face. They share air as her lips touch his. Re-igniting a lustful need, they once shared. "You do not value my love or adoration; you only want to toy with my emotions,"

"Henry..." her heart beats faster; his aggression arouses a longing in her long dormant. "I wanna be good, I wanna be yours, but you're so distant to me Henry. You return and never came to see me... what am I to do with a man that does not care anymore?" A tear well up in her eyes and compassion or is it lust, now sweeps over Henry. Charlotte senses that he is under her spell when she spies Alonzo and the Jacksons approaching out of the corner of her eye. She watched earlier as Henry kissed Anna's hand and now sees her as a pure threat to the marriage as if her own behaviors were not.

Unbeknownst to Charlotte, Anna too has been watching their entire conversation from afar. She could not make out their words but Anna does suspect something terribly wrong with the relationship. Moreover, she aims to play her part in its demise.

Charlotte sees the three coming towards them, her lips press to Henry's and she steals a kiss.

'This should ward off my competition until I can bed my husband in a proper fashion,' she thinks not noticing that Anna has dropped her head from the view. Henry is furious at her public display of affection, pulls away. But, too late; Anna sees everything. Alonzo arrives to interrupt them.

"So sorry to intrude, the Jacksons and I are taking a short ride into DC and will return before supper." Anna smiles at Henry drawing a menacing grin from Charlotte. Freddie tips his hat and the three hurry off to a waiting carriage.

Anna turns one last time to catch a glimpse of Henry, to find him doing the same. Once in the carriage, she turns to Freddie, "She doesn't seem so bad, I mean, if that's what you like," Freddie rolls his eyes and Alonzo bursts out in laughter.

"Well you said a mouthful,"

Henry and Charlotte take their leave as well, walking arm in arm, they head back to Edwards home. Charlotte takes one last jab at Anna, the pleasant distraction in Henry's eye.

"Well, I guess the men in Rhode Island prefer their niggas as white as can be," Henry does not play into her pettiness.

"I guess."

HOME OF EDWARD MASSEY FIVE HOURS LATER

Henry is pacing back and forth anticipating the arrival

of Alonzo and the Jacksons. Seated in the kitchen are Edward and fair-skinned neighbor, George Chichester. It is odd for George to be in the house when Edward is home, he usually will talk to Edward in the fields or in town. However, he comes to the house to visit daily when the elder Massey is not about. Henry does not trust the man.

It is sundown before Charlotte calls him into the bedroom. Her intent is obvious as he walks through the door. She wants to reassert herself within his life and his bed. Clad in a skimpy undergarment she walks him to their bed. Edward and George continue their discussion, but George is preoccupied with Henry's disappearance.

On this warm spring evening, a single open window provides fresh air and a breeze. Charlotte has two candles and a kerosene lamp for illumination. However, she sees fit to use just a candle tonight.

Henry is not taking the bait, "What will this solve Charlotte? You must change your ways, no alcohol or pharmaceuticals, and no more flirting with men as if I didn't exist," he walks out of a side door Edward built so that Charlotte could come and go as she pleases. It made access to her room hidden from those approaching from the main road.

Henry leans against the outside of the house and ponders necessary life decisions yet to come. He hears the wheels of a carriage approaching and steadies his heart and thoughts. Charlotte hears them too. She stands at her window still clad in just her undergarment. Dusk gives way to nightfall, so that only a silhouette is visible from the road.

Anna peers from the carriage as it approaches the house. Charlotte sees her and thinks of how to sew divisive seeds in a fertile patch of infatuation she fears is developing. She moans loud enough for people to hear in the house. Then she adds a one sided dialog for those curious ears now in tune.

"Oh Henry, I waited so long my lover. Give it fill me until I am overflowing," Henry hears and turns but the door is locked. Frustrated he walks to the front of the house. Charlotte's torso is visible from the road. She moves her hips as if someone is behind her. "Henry, Henry, yes, yes," she screams.

Anna puts her hand to her mouth at both the audio and visual stimulation. Alonzo and Freddie are at a loss for words until they see Henry walking to the carriage. A sight Charlotte does not.

"Well I'll be, so how are you in the throes of passion 60 feet away, and standing in front of us?" Alonzo shakes his head, as Anna looks on puzzled.

"One might say my wife has a vivid imagination. Does anyone fancy a game of cards at Alonzo's?"

"I most certainly do after this charade," Freddie's attempts at levity win the night. Henry enters the carriage and it rolls on to Alonzo's home two miles away. Charlotte realizes too late that Henry is long gone. She sits back on her bed and contemplates on whether or not to invite George in later. First, she has a drink.

Henry returns to Rhode Island a month later. A relationship blossoms between him and Anna but Henry does not commit emotionally because he is still married to Charlotte. He receives a letter from Alonzo informing him that a close family member is sick and that Charlotte is 9 months pregnant and due any day.

Thoughts run through his head, 'Things don't add up right,' but he had relations a full month before he left, if she were pregnant, he would have known way before this late in the pregnancy. He makes plans to return to Va, but it will be another month before he finally does.

Henry arrives at the train station and heads directly

to Edward's home where Charlotte still lives. He enters the house and sees the baby. Henry is not happy. The baby is much lighter than Henry, given that Charlotte's complexion is light brown.

Henry assumes that the baby is at least as light as he is if not darker. The baby looks as if the father was white, and definitely not Henry's child. At least that is what he thought, and most that saw the child assume the same.

He knows that Charlotte is lying, in order for the baby to be his; he had to be here nine months ago which he was not, and besides the baby is white.

Henry visits his relative and returns to Rhode Island. He will file for divorce from Charlotte and marry Anna within the year.

The New Reformers

Over five years have passed since his divorce from Charlotte (1883) and later marriage to Anna. Henry is a well-respected member of Pawtucket, RI. He serves as a patrol officer for the city's police department and is a delegate of the National Association of True Reformers.

The treatment and condition of blacks, a decade after reconstruction ends, is a major concern for Henry. He will voice his concern and show his support at the convention in Richmond later this month. But, today, duty calls.

It is a normal day for Officer Massey. Henry is out on patrol when he hears a noise and the familiar sound of a police officer's whistle.

"Stop him," the officer shouts pointing to a man running through the bustling street. Henry turns on a dime and moves to help in the capture of a felon. He moves with speed and purpose like a Cheetah chasing its prey on the Serengeti.

"Henry, give chase I will cut him off near Stearns Street," the officer shouts. Henry nods and runs after the man now in full stride. The felon knocks over an apple cart and two patrons, Henry hurdles the fallen cart and the patrons sprawled in the street.

"You get'em Henry," screams the vendor assisting his customers.

Henry has no time to acknowledge the man, he is hell bent on capturing the felon before he gets to the train tracks where vagrants and hobos frequent. He is fast. Henry is faster. He dismisses the need to match his adversary's zigzags and instead focuses on maintaining his speed.

The fugitive, now only 10 feet from Henry's grasp,

takes a wide turn, narrowing the distance to just one stride. He reaches not for his collar, but for the lagging foot, tripping the man who hurls head long into the street. Henry walks over to him and kneels, "I won't beat you, but old Bob doesn't run," Henry removes handcuffs from his coat. "Bob will give you a licking you won't soon forget, for making him run today yes indeed."

The short and stumpy officer shows up minutes later breathing heavy but still able to give one order.

"Henry you hold this bastard up for me," Henry looks at Bob who is out of breath and sweating profusely.

"You sure you wanna beat on this one? He's a good foot taller than you Bob," the fugitive is taller than Henry too, who stands six feet. He holds the man up for Bob.

"Sir, you rat bastard you," taking deep breaths. "I arrest you in the name of the Pawtucket Police Department," Bob usually hauls off and belts a prisoner in the face. Considering the height of this one, Bob's intent is to demean, and make sure he runs no more. He gives the man a swift kick in the groin.

"Well that's new Bob," Henry laughs at his supervisor's method. This same fugitive will end up dismembered on the train tracks six years later. Henry will find the body. Or whats left.

NEW REFORMERS NATIONAL MEETING RICHMOND

Freddie accompanies Anna and Henry to the national convention. He is curious how the organization will address lynching on a massive scale. Also on the agenda are the unfair racist business practices that target black business owners, and the black codes which imprison both men and women for being unemployed.

Henry takes these as his own cause. He listens to the orator's call for active member recruitment. There are pleas for blacks to take ownership of their own commerce and education in the communities where they live. Henry leaves Richmond to join Anna in Falls Church and begins openly recruiting new members against the advice of Alonzo.

"I see you're just going to ignore my advice and post bills around the church and market. The attention you get is not what you want son,"

"Alonzo I have heeded your words and only passed these around the church. I doubt folks will even read them,"

"If they can read that is," Alonzo shakes his head in disbelief at the younger Massey, who does not appreciate the social climate in the south. "I will keep close still the same. Folks know I always have my rifle handy," he holds up a 'Henry rifle' his prize from the war.

TWO DAYS LATER

The day comes and Henry readies the meeting in the Alfred Street Baptist Church. He checks his timepiece several times to see if it has stopped.

'Where is everybody?' he thinks to himself. An hour later, he walks out of the church and sees two men mulling around a block away. They were too scared to come to the meeting. Henry finds out that a group of white businessmen have discouraged blacks in Alexandria from taking part. Henry is livid, and this anger sets him on a dangerous course.

ALEXANDRIA VA EARLIER THAT DAY

Lenard Colby owns a small dry goods store a mile from the Alfred Street Church on the outskirts of the 'bottoms'. He opens his store during reconstruction and serves both whites and blacks alike. His major competition sits just a quarter mile away, and a former overseer, Charles Whitney owns it.

Colby's shop is cheap, fast, and dependable. But, his competition, sees this as an affront and lets anyone who will listen know.

Lenard has a wife, Mazey. She is a light-skinned mulatto and was a domestic servant on the plantation Whitney oversaw. He often trolls and stalks her, looking for one more chance to resume relations from over a decade ago.

The tension between the three comes to a head when Lenard (39) confronts Whitney (55). An argument ensues and Whitney falls, the pregnant Mazey pulls her husband aside.

"That right there is gonna cost you boy," Whitney threatens.

"Sir he didn't mean nothing by it, please just leave us be," Mazey pleads but Lenard's anger takes over his words and sense.

"You stay away from me and mines cracker," and that ends the conversation.

THE BOTTOMS ALEXANDRIA 9PM

A mob of angry white men with scarves covering their mouths, (and others not ashamed of the association) march through the 'bottoms'. They torch Lenard's store and drag him and Mazey out into the middle of the street. Henry is still canvassing for recruits when he stumbles upon the scene.

"There go that nigga from the north. Get him too!" they subdue Henry before he can retreat. He receives a beating but not as savage as Lenard's, for Henry only dared to organize blacks where Lenard dared to put his hands on a white man. No matter how justified that will always get you lynched. But other factors are in play.

Numerous assaults (such as lynching) during this era of the 'New Negro' (first generation born free and not slaves) have little to do with race but speak more to whites re-establishing themselves in the class structure. Blacks are moving into their neighborhoods, displacing them in the workplace, and attaining higher education in big numbers.

They opine over blacks in direct competition to their business interests, subvert, and intimidate them until they close. In other areas, they place laws to hamstring the abilities of blacks to gain loans, housing, and education. And with planters no longer owning blacks, they're not a valuable commodity, so brutal and savage assaults have become common place.

Henry steps right into this hornet's nest. Mazey, (five months pregnant) suffers humiliation from the men that rip her clothes from her body, revealing her status. Something she and her husband were shouting at them for the entire miserable event. This halts more beatings, but does not hinder her rape in the middle of the street.

Henry, held at gunpoint, cannot raise his head to witness her dishonor at the hands of Whitney and others. Lenard is alive but cannot see the raping of his wife, but hears her screams, chilling and mournful. Those sounds haunt him for the rest of a life that will end soon.

The heat and humidity of this early June evening, is oppressive. Henry finds it hard to breathe, but he can hear just fine. His oppressors are deciding to either lynch or burn the men. They do both.

A noose hangs around both of their necks as their captors take them to the nearest lamppost. Four blocks away, Alonzo is loading his Henry rifle, when Freddie bolts into his hotel room.

"Where is your cousin, I overheard something disturbing in a bar a few miles away?"

"Did you now? Are you playing white again?"

"Let's say I get in where I fit in and leave it at that sir. Now where is Henry?" Freddie's face shows his concern and Alonzo worries too.

"I haven't seen him in over an hour. We were sposed to meet back here after he did his recruiting," the two look out of the window to see people running to their homes.

"Now this doesn't look good."

"So where is the store owned by a Lenard-."

"Colby, his store is north from here,"

"The same direction these people are running from. If that rifle is loaded lets be on our way. Henry may need us," the two run out of the hotel and towards Colby's store and the lynch mob.

Alonzo and Freddie catch up with a gaggle of men who have grabbed Henry and are set to lynch him. Freddie thinks fast and writes out a promissory note and Alonzo signs Henry's name. The two race to the crowd.

"Fire off a round and then take aim at the man holding Henry," they step forward. A single shot rings out. "Cease and desist your savagery or my man will take you out one by one. You know he is a crack shot," the men mistake Freddie as white. He demands compensation if they plan on killing Henry.

"This nigger owes me 500 dollars," Freddie reaches into his vest pocket. "Here is the note and his signature. Now if any of you white men want to deprive me of my right to recompense, then we will be at the judge's house tonight. Hang this boy and you pay me, don't pay me, no hanging," the men look at each other and one shouts back at Freddie.

"What are you some kind of Yankee carpetbagger sir?"

"No are you mad? I was born in Fauquier County. My family still owns land here and in Maryland. After the war, we sold many parcels of land and invested in shipping," Freddie walks right up to the man holding Henry. He lifts Henry's chin to assess his injuries. "Our investments in shipping explain my current residence in Rhode Island. We are selling off our properties here, with the exceptions of lands still held in trust, family estates etcetera. I came to see for myself the land this man offers to purchase in this note," Freddie is playing to the audience and Alonzo believes he is better suited as a white man than a colored one.

"I do not covet land in Virginia, hard to manage from Rhode Island so you see why I am so inclined to sell. But I would gladly forsake this man's offer to any of you for 500 dollars," the men look back and forth, Whitney, the chief instigator, is busy trying to get more of Mazey. "Will someone please tell that rapist to stop, it is very off putting. Once again, lynch mob, no money no hanging. In addition, I will not be party to you forcing him to sign over a deed under duress. Nope this has to be legal and above board," Freddie winks at Alonzo.

One man yanks the rope around Henry's neck pulling him to the ground. Alonzo trembles steadies his weapon and moans. Freddie quiets his nerves.

"Now I don't give two shits about no niggers and their meetings or how you do things here in the common-wealth. But the white man's laws are on my side, so if none of you have my 500 dollars," none of the men budge. "Right, then please oblige me and let this boy go so I can tend to my affairs." The men look at Freddie and give him the rope.

"See he has no more meetings while he is here, church included." Freddie and Alonzo pick up Henry and hurry away. Freddie sees Mazey lying in the middle of the street naked. "Well we still got this one," a man walks over to a dying Lenard Colby and shoots him four times, and twice in the head. His body hangs from the lamppost as an example for blacks remember their place.

Lenard Colby dared to run a competitive business but his pride and ego would not allow him to let sexual harassment go unchecked. Pride is something Mazey had long left aside. She gave Whitney what he wanted after the incident to appease his anger and save Lenard. His sexual appetite for her was satisfied for the moment, but not his hatred for an enterprising new Negro.

The three go back towards the hotel. Alonzo runs inside and gathers their things. He puts the men in a coach for Union Station and then heads back to retrieve Anna. They (Henry, Anna, and Freddie) board the first train back north in the am. The entire traumatic event unnerves Henry.

Freddie assures him that he was not the catalyst of the lynching he was just there. Yet guilt grips the young Massey. He never takes to the bottle, however, the experience of a near lynching spiral him into bouts of depression for the rest of his life.

The Negress Dies

From the time of her release from prison until her death, Melvina entertained people and ran her brothel. However, she assumes a low profile for bootlegging, and her competitors appreciate the sentiments. Melvina's age restricts her to just keeping whores in line. In 1908, she entertains Marshall Bullock prior to him becoming Warden of Yellowstone.

He enters the Crystal Palace and kisses Melvina's hand.

"Seth Bullock I am so glad to see you. Come, give me a hug," which the aging Madame offers her guest.

"Melvina Massey, striking as the day is long,"

"Oh, come now you know I am an old maid not worth a poke,"

"Madame I never want to separate a woman from her delusions, but there are numerous men willing to pay for a poke I am sure,"

"And you would be accurate... not to separate a woman from her delusions," the two share a moment and a shot of blackberry brandy. "So what brings you to Fargo of all places?"

"I am heading into the Yellowstone and want to visit with acquaintances I may not lay eyes on again," Melvina feels every letter in his words.

"Yes we are getting up in years dear, but I am sure there is something festering inside of your brain you wants to ask me,"

"Oh you are never one to beat around the bush. Your deductive reasoning is beyond compare fair lady. Yes I have a question for you, and you are not obliged to answer," Melvina motions for another round and eases back in her chair.

"Out with it then dear sweet man,"

"Have you ever seen an Appaloosa Melvina?"

"That's a horse right?"

"Yes a unique breed, one that improves others when you interbreed them. I have an amazing stag on my ranch. Power and grace over every inch of his body. I could watch him forever. He reminds me of you in a way. Graceful and strong,"

"So I remind you of a horse? A male horse at that, am I wrong to sense a question coming soon?"

"Almost there my clever host. I like to stir my coffee after I add the cream," the Marshal takes another sip of his Brandy and smiles realizing that he is drinking in a dry state. "Throughout our entire acquaintance there is just one thing that baffles my mind and ego,"

"Well?" another round of drinks arrives and they toast to the bygone west.

"How in the hell did you do it?"

"Do what Marshal or Warden?"

"Don't play coy with me Melvina," Melvina stands and walks over to her distinguished guest. She stands behind his chair and bends to whisper in his ear.

"Perspectives change depending on where one sits,"

"Or stands," Bullock drinks his Brandy.

"Now why in the world would a person on the wrong side of the law ever divulge her secrets to a lawman?"

"Considering I am now a Warden of Yellowstone, you're safe, unless you intend to run a whore house and bootleg in my territory," Melvina kisses Bullock on the ear and sits.

"Once again I tell you of a thing. Where do I begin?"

"The beginning?"

"Oh no dear, we are at the end. Let us skip to the epilogue. There is enough to satisfy your hunger,"

"Fair enough, another Brandy." Their drinks arrive and the mulatto Madame spins a tale of intrigue and clan-

---

The Color of Power

destine activities all under the Cass County prosecutor's nose.

"They were only partly right about me, but that had nothing to do with my color or gender. Maybe it did, but my ego says it is more to do with their ineptitude than anything else, well that and their racist views." Bullock raises a glass to her last statement.

Melvina reveals to him that a relation of hers comes to visit three years before the Crystal Palace fire. Franklin Jackson visits Fargo and stays at her establishment. He shares interesting news learned during his trip through Minnesota.

Melvina provides a picture of the young Jackson for the Marshal's curiosity. The first thing he notices is the most obvious.

"I guess there is a bountiful amount of near-white people in your family huh Madame Massey?"

"You would be correct," Melvina takes the photo of young Freddie back to its place on the mantle. She describes what Freddie discovers from men assuming he is white.

The time is 1889 in the spring and Freddie is visiting relatives in St Paul. There he hears of his wonderful mother-in-law Madame Massey. It was strange to hear of a black brothel owner among so many white men, but Freddie said 'they had no clue'. An evening of talk and boasting and the young New Englander comes away with information of mines, smuggling, and there not being enough booze for the booming businesses in Moorehead.

"You had good information, but it was 1889, too late to stake a claim in Portage, or in Moorehead,"

"Oh contraire Mon frère," Melvina takes one more sip of her Brandy.

What Freddie divulges to Melvina, she takes advantage of in every possible way. Melvina sets up a laundry business in Rat Portage, near the mines. However, just like in Chicago, the laundry is a fraud. Her girls get key information on claims and shipments and she cashes that in for access. She negotiates with Canadian alcoholic beverage suppliers and establishes her own smuggling routes.

"Interesting so you were set up to sell in North -."

"No silly man. North Dakota was only a route, not the destination. Moorehead is where I made my money,"

"I am missing something. So what are these routes?"

"Have you ever heard of the Underground Railroad?" the Marshal nods his head.

"Yes vaguely,"

"Well I purchased property and modest homes along various routes from Canada, through North Dakota, and into Minnesota. Each property has its purpose. The property and homes we own outright. We store alcohol and provisions along the route, moving the goods from one place to another. The homesteaders are lookouts along the roads and all they need do is to hang a lantern if no officers are near. We also devised other methods based on the laundry hanging in their yards. This confuses the law each time they believe they have us figured out we change,"

"So how does one make an order with you?"

"Back when I was in business, the Palace is where the transactions took place. However, I spent much time in Moorehead taking orders over dinner too. Well may be more than a little,"

"My goodness Melvina so what in tarnation was you up to in the Palace?"

"The Palace was only a front; I made my money off of the booze, but never sold much within these walls. Only pokes." A realization comes over the Marshal. Melvina Massey was exactly what the Cass County prosecutor said she was a bootlegger. Yet they had no idea how successful she was as one.

In their minds, she was a white madam running a coon dive and selling the occasional illegal drink. Then they discover her identity and she becomes the scourge of the west.

The two spend another hour together before the Marshal says his goodbye. He will never see her alive again.

Melvina spends the next years avoiding extortion and other civil issues. Her health fades.

MAY 4 1911 FARGO

After many months of sickness, Melvina entertains a few close associates over a week and dies. Her last words to those present at her side were simple.

"Take what you need, but leave the rest for Henry," the Crystal Palace is ransacked, and the County closes it until her family arrives.

On his ranch in the Yellowstone, Seth Bullock receives message of her demise. He walks out to his stables and releases his prize Appaloosa.

"Run free."

Newspapers in Fargo share a similar headline 'The Negress is dead'.

1912 FARGO

Henry fends off creditors for months and finally gives up any claims to property Melvina owned. He wins access to the Palace (which he has owned since 1907) and takes inventory of his mother's belongings. He and Anna head back to Minnesota. Over the next few years the once vibrant and active police officer, withdraws into deeper depression. Then in 1916 after seeing a black man lynched; Henry suffers an anxiety attack. It triggers an aneurism, and he dies three days later.

Anna does not fare much better, no record of death, but she dies shortly after Henry.

Union Station

After her father's death, Jane Elizabeth AKA Fascination leaves RI for New York. She is only there for a short while before coming back to Virginia. Fascination is the third oldest of the surviving children, and the one who enjoys colorful language. She shares this trait with her grandmother Melvina. The young woman probably learns it on her many trips to the Palace.

Her train pulls into Union Station, and she takes her time looking at the numerous shops before boarding her next train into Virginia. Fascination is a tall striking woman not as jaw dropping as her grandmother Melvina. However, she still turns heads.

While waiting for her next train, a porter catches her eye. She smiles back at him and he tips his hat. A white man calls for help with his bags and the young Abraham Smith ignores him and walks to Fascination.

"Ma'am if I may, where are you headed today?"

"Yes you may, but I am not a ma'am. Please call me Jane if you must call me anything,"

"Jane, is that what your people call you, it's not a name befitting such a -."

"Fascination,"

"Yes you are fascinating, but I was -."

"No they call me Fascination, I am Fascination Massey, of the Virginia, Rhode Island, and New York Masseys," Abraham cannot take his eyes off of her face.

"Yes you are, indeed," the two spend the next 15 minutes talking and flirting. Numerous men grow frustrated with Abraham the porter who is not doing his job. The four o'clock train for Falls Church pulls into the station. Abraham knows if he lets this woman leave he may never see her again. So he takes a gamble. He scoops up her bags and runs with them.

"Hey," Her train is arriving and this handsome young man has just run off with her bags. She gives chase. "Come back here you son of a bitch. That's my momma's bag,"

Abraham runs out the station and across the street. Fascination is trailing behind, cussing, and trying not to tear her dress. Abraham ducks into a sandwich shop and watches her run by. He eases out and takes two steps before he comes face to face with one angry Massey.

"Fascination let me explain," she swings at the six foot Abraham and misses his head by a mile falling into his arms and over her bags.

"What are you laughing at you lousy good for nothing -." He kisses her.

"I didn't want you to leave just yet, I had this terrible fear I would never see you again," his kiss catches Fascination off guard but she is no fool. She slaps his face.

"I appreciate your efforts Mr. Smith, but if you intend for me to sit around with you for another hour, your kisses better be up to par," another kiss from Abraham follows which is more to her liking. "When is the next train?"

They spend the next hour together and Abraham accompanies her to Falls Church. Abraham and Fascination will marry shortly thereafter beginning another chapter in the Massey saga as young Fascination is destined to be part of history herself. Life is better with love in abundance.

Fascination Massey

ShaRon Downing

ARLINGTON VIRGINIA 2010

The oldest son, of Abraham and Fascination Smith, Abraham Jr., (AKA baby brother his sisters cut it short to just Bay), is suffering from a long illness. ShaRon Downing and her sister, come to pay their respects to the uncle who always gives a dollar. They sit for an afternoon reminiscing over pictures and stories from his youth. He tells funny anecdotes about their Aunt Cecilia and Uncle Eddie, the family in Rhode Island and Virginia. Then, as the day grows longer, he tires. ShaRon and her cousin are about to leave and then Uncle Bay Brother gives them one last story. It is a short one, just nine words. A gleam comes in his eye and the two women lean closer.

"Well you know there's a madam in our family."

They look at each other in disbelief thinking that the illness has made him delusional. But each can sense that the man is lucid in his tone and delivery. He goes on to say that, the madam in question was his great grandmother. He gives no name and closes his eyes. The two sisters discuss this odd occurrence on the way home. ShaRon stores it away until she meets Brandon Massey a few years later.

Sha'Ron Downing (left) is the 4xGreat Granddaughter of Melvina. Her 2xGreat Grandmother was Fascination Massey of Va.

Brandon Massey finds his 3xgreatgrandfather Henry Massey searching for Melvina.

Daddy what you doin?

Brandon Massey is driving with his aunt Loretta Massey. His mind is on a conversation he had with his daughter. She asks him 'daddy what you doin?' as little ones so often do. Brandon was deep in thought on his ancestors and the family's past.

He turns to his daughter, "Daddy is thinking about our family,"

"Oh ok," and off she went. Little did the child know that her brief interruption would serve as a catalyst for her father's new quest. The next day he asks his aunty about the family, and she begins to list the brothers and sisters, of her father Milton Coyle Massey. One of the siblings was Fascination. Brandon questions if that was her true name, and his aunty replies "Yes we used to call her aunt Fassi."

Brandon does a quick online search, which directs him to Ancestry.com. A posting by a ShaRon Downing is the number one result. She is also looking for a Fascination Massey. They quickly discover that they are third cousins.

Brandon has no luck on finding information on his family, so he focuses on the story ShaRon shared about a madam. He searches online for any data on a 'madam Massey' and prostitution, and that is when it got complicated.

Brandon sets out to answer the following questions about Melvina, he brings ShaRon, and a little known author (James Lee Nathan III) along.

1. Where was Melvina Massey born and raised?

2. Why was Melvina absent during her son's upbringing?

3. Was Melvina's features such that she could easily pass for white? Or was she noticeably of African descent?
4. What led Melvina Massey to the "sporting life"?
5. Why is the life of Melvina's son, Henry Massey, apparently so different from hers?
6. Why and when did Melvina decide to go to Fargo, North Dakota?
7. How wealthy was Melvina?
8. What member of the Loudoun Grays fathered Melvina's son?
9. Why did Melvina marry Charles Rae? Did she love him? Or was it strictly business?
10. Was the city of Fargo out to get Melvina and why?
11. Given Melvina's wealth how did her son, Henry Massey, come out to be destitute?
12. Was our Melvina the same who sued Louis H.P. Davis, the father of the first African American Army General?
13. What's the connection to Rhode Island?
14. What can we do to discover more about Melvina?

These are the questions this ebook and paperback have sought to answer. How did we do?

Videos on the search for Melvina:

Finding Melvina Intro - http://youtu.be/qJV3WAD6ajQ Finding Melvina Massey - Intro youtube

In this introduction to "Finding Melvina Massey", Roshawn Massey gives us a very brief history of Melvina Massey.

Finding Melvina I - http://youtu.be/eU8LDBBME4Q Finding Melvina Massey - Episode 1 youtube

Episode one of "Finding Melvina Massey" takes us to the Hjemkomst Center in Moorhead, MN to check out the Taboo Exhibit.

Finding Melvina II - http://youtu.be/0prO5KucRgA
Finding Melvina Massey - Episode 2 youtube

Episode Two of "Finding Melvina Massey" takes us to the Fargo City Hall and Cass County Courthouse in search of property records for Melvina Massey.

Finding Melvina III - http://youtu.be/Ua8N6vZ6UmA
Finding Melvina Massey - Episode 3 youtube

In this episode we took a closer look at Melvina's homes and a peek at her run-ins with the law.

Finding Melvina IV - http://youtu.be/wsB3VPOI3G4
Finding Melvina Massey - Episode 4 youtube

The final episode that details Melvina Massey's final resting place.

Melvina - The Color of Power - http://youtu.be/SZ3oRht_-DXM

Henry Massey Jr.

Rhode Island Masseys. Henry's descendants.

Milton Coyle Massey

Transcript of Divorce

The following depositions (as transcribed from the original court documents) support Henry's claim that the baby was not his, based on its color and Charlotte's full term pregnancy (meaning he was not in the state).

**Transcribed by Brandon Massey **

NOTE: content within parens means I have guessed at what the content was.

Content with question marks means I have no idea.

To the Hon James Keith judge of the Circuit Court of Fairfax County –

Your Orator Henry Massey respectfully showeth unto your honor that he was married to one Charlotte Scott on the 25th of December 1879. That afterwards in the time a child was born to them but it lived only a short time and died. That your Orator lived with his said wife until sometime in April 1881. That he then saw that further cohabitation would only result as the past had done in nothing but regrets and unhappy disagreements, which her course of conduct provoked. That his (?) and solicitations to change her behavior were entirely unheeded and disregarded. That wearied and despairing of ever being able to effect any reform in her. He left her and went to live in Rhode Island. That he remained there continuously until June 17, 1882 where the sickness of a relative called him home. That during his stay he went to see her hoping that she might have reflected on her past wayward course and that she would now be willing to discharge those duties which he would ever have been too happy to have her perform. But he found that no change had taken place whatever in her feelings and that she had wandered still further from him than before. Painfully aware that all further association between them would be impossible he returned to Rhode Island on the 6th of July, 1882. That he did not return to Virginia until February 1883 that he there discovered that his suspicions about her had only been too true, and that she had become the mother of another child on the 29th of January 1883. That those familiar with such matters informed your Orator that said child had been produced in the regular period of gestation and that it was what is called a full-term child. Your Orator avers that in the course of nature it was utterly impossible for him to have been the father of said child and that said child must have been conceived in or about the last of April 1882 at which time your Orator was in Rhode Island. Your Orator avers that it has ever been his wish to live in peace and happiness and to enjoy those pleasures in which domestic life is usually so fruitful. But that to live further with his said wife will now be impossible, as he could never more be happy in the company or society of one so lost to every of virtue and propriety. Your Orator therefore prays that the said Charlotte Massey his wife may be made a party defendant to this bill, and required to answer the same on oath. That your Orator may be divorced a (vinculo) matrimonie from his said wife, and that such other and general relief may be granted your Orator as to (equity) may seem (meet) and right.

And your Orator will pray (to)
Henry Massey
WITNESS ALONZO MASSEY
Henry Massey
Vs
Charlotte Massey
No witnesses appearing in (obedience) to summons on this day 15th May 1883 to which time the notices + summons were (returnable), the taking of depositions is (con––) to May 23rd 1883.

(SOME PERSON'S SIGNATURE)

May 23rd 1883

The depositions of Alonzo Massey (D McLeod).

Taken to Fairfax County at his office at Fairfax C.H.

May 23 1883 – to be read in a (suit) in (Enlgish)... (in said court on behalf of complaint) in which (suit) Henry Massey is plaintiff + Charlotte Massey is defendant .

(Pre???) Thomas + (Keith) for plaintiff.

No appearance for defendant.

Alonzo Massey being duly sworn deposes + says 1st Keith for (complainant).

What is your age, residence + occupation?

(avers): "I am about 38 years old. I live at Falls Church + am a (laborer).

"Are you [acquainted] with Henry Massey the plaintiff, how long have you known him + what is his reputation in the neighborhood? How far did you live from him?"

[avers]: "I have known him for over 15 years. His reputation was very good. I lived about 2 ½ miles from him."

"Do you know whether or not the plaintiff Henry Massey has (married) the defendant Charlotte Massey + did they live happily together?"

(avers): "I do know they were married. I can't tell (except) that I (heard) they did. I don't know it of my own knowledge."

"About what time did he leave the (state) + what time did he return?"

(avers): "He left in 1881 + did not return till the latter part of June 1882

"When was the last child of Charlotte Massey born + how did it appear?"

(avers): "About the better part of January 1883. It was well-developed."

"What was the color of the child?"

(avers): "It was very (light/bright)."

"What is the color of Henry Massey + the color of Charlotte Massey?"

(avers): "Henry is pretty light + Charlotte is brown skinned."

"(????) That child too light colored for Henry Massey's child?"

(avers): "It is pretty light colored for him and This
Signed Alonzo Massey
Witness By (someone's signature)
(1 day 50 ch ??? by HWi)
WITNESS DR. WILFRED McLEOD

[D. Wilfred McLeod] being duly sworn deposes and says by plaintiff's atty

1. "What is your age, residence + occupation?"

(avers) "I am (forty), I live near Vienna + I am a physician."

"Have you or not had (considerable ???) in (obstetrical) cases

(avers): "I have – in hospitals. I have been practicing for seven years."

"Did you (deliver) (the) defendant Charlotte Massey of a child + if so at what time?"

(avers): "I did on or about the 29th of January 1883."

"Do you (not) consider the child as having been born in the (regular) course of gestation or a full term child?"

(avers): "I do think it was a full term child and there were no indications of premature delivery + the child was well developed.

And further (saith was)
Witness (attendance) Wilfred McLeod

Making the Case the Historical Melvina Massey

Fargo had its fair share of illegal entertainment, including prostitution. Early Fargoans did not try to abolish prostitution, but rather generated city income by fining brothels a pre-determined amount. This house at 201 Third Street North, was owned by Malvina Massey, an African-American madam. Black entertainers visiting Fargo, who were frequently barred from hotels and boarding houses, usually ended up staying with Massey. (NDIRS, FHc, 106-2)

Crystal Palace

This was the 'Crown Jewel' of Melvina's brothel empire in Fargo North Dakota.

INFORMATION ON MIMA AND OTHERS

The following are the collected notes between Brandon Massey and Ms. Debbie Robison, who collaborated with Brandon in tracing Melvina's father and possible grandmother.

We are confidant (within 90% probability) that Mima is Melvina's grandmother. The Ruffin connection is too compelling to ignore.

September 7, 2016

"I tried to find out how John Ross came to own Melvina who had a child named James H in Loudoun County.

I have not figured that out yet, but it may have been through purchase rather than inheritance.

I checked the 1850 Federal Slave Census for John Ross, but could not find a girl the correct age, so maybe he acquired her sometime between 1850 and 1858.

There is an earlier record in 1849/1850 for a Melvina in Loudoun County in the will books for George Cuthbert Powell.

The Powell's live in Middleburg, Loudoun County, VA near the border with Fauquier County.

The following link provides the names and ages of the slaves owned by George Cuthbert Powell at his death. Melvina, a 13-year-old girl, is included. This is about the correct age for Melvina Massey. The Fiduciary References can be found

here:www.loudoun.gov/DocumentCenter/View/120934

There was a slave auction on Wednesday, November 7, 1849 at "The Hill" the late residence of Geo. Cuthbert Powell, decd. near Middleburg. This information is from an original record on file at the Thomas Balch Library in Leesburg. The results of the sale are recorded in the Loudoun County Will Books. James H. Simpson (the H stands for Hendley) purchased Peyton, Lavinia, and Washington. Then he purchased Melvina and Charles (who was a 6-year-old boy).

[A possible brother?] James H. Simpson was a merchant and moved for a short time to Fairfax County.

'He became encumbered of debt' based on the court cases available here: www.lva.virginia.gov/chancery/?_-ga=1.19342328.1760558823.1447197407

In 1862, James H. Simpson moved to Texas bringing with him slaves that were born in Virginia.

[hmmm] I saw on your Massey Family website that Melvina Massey had niece named Margaret Ruffin. I found that her maiden name is Margaret Massey and that her husband was Willis Ruffin. In the 1870 census, she is in Washington, DC. In the 1910 census, she is in Manhattan. Her son's (Ellsworth Ruffin) Social Security claim provides his parents' names as Margaret Massie and Willis Ruffin.

The claim states that Ellsworth was born in Rectortown F, Va. [which I think means Rectortown, Fauquier County, Virginia] Rectortown is near Middleburg. So...Margaret Massey mush be the daughter of one of Melvina Massey's brothers or she is a daughter of an unmarried sister, perhaps a brother or sister who moved to Rectortown prior to emancipation. Robert Beverly purchased a girl named Louisa from the Powell auction. He lived at 'Kinloch Farm' near 'The Plains' which is near Rectortown. This might be a possibility to pursue. I have to run...I'll send you a couple of documents via email.

Oh, and I just saw that George Cuthbert Powell's widow, Marietta, moved to Upperville, Fauquier County after he died.

So many possibilities for research." Debbie

Later that day

"Oh my goodness, this is all opening up possibilities. I found Washington Massie, b. abt 1844 in Warrenton, Fauquier County in 1844. He is the correct age for the slave named Washington listed in George Cuthbert Powell's inventory. And there is the family of James Massey in Upperville (where George's widow moved with slaves) in the 18710 census. He was born c. 1810.

Later... Correction to last post...Washington was listed in the 1870 census in Warrenton. He wasn't necessarily born there."

September 8, 2016

"The 1900 census for Maragrate (Margaret) Ruffin shows her living in DC with her sister Blanche Macy (Massey?) I find a Blance Massey in the 1880 census as the daughter of James and Grace Massey of Upperville, Fauquier County. So... if Margaret Ruffin is the niece of Melvina AND Blanche Massey is the sister of Margaret Ruffin AND Blanche's parents are James and Grace Massey THEN you would expect that James Massey of Upperville is a brother to Melvina. (Or Grace Massey is a sister of Melvina and James took Grace's surname."

September 11, 2016

"I've had some breakthroughs. I have got the family back to Mima, a slave owned by Moore Fauntleroy Carter (1771-1820) in Fauquier County, VA. For the names of Moore's slaves, see Fauquier County chancery case 1830-134. Judith Carter, widow of Moore and mother of Judith F Carter, retained most of the family slaves and managed the property, including Mima.

This case has plats of the land. Moore lived near Delaplane and Rectortown in Fauquier County. (Just south of Upperville and Middleburg) In 1845, Judith Carter's slaves needed to be sold at auction as the result of a court-case for debt. By this time, Mima has had children and they are named in Fauquier County chancery case 1846-034. Mima's children are Jane, Edward, John, and Lucian. William is also included in the sale, but not specifically as one of Mima's children. Jane, Edward, John, and Lucian were purchased by James Blackwell, a family member by marriage. Judith got to retain the slaves. William, however, was not purchased by Blackwell. The children are referred to as 'family slaves.'

I'm guessing that means they are blood relations to the Carter family since they are indicated in the census as mulattos. I believe that Mima's son Edward is your Edward (father of Melvina). I believe that he fathered children with a woman named Caroline who lived on an adjacent property. She may have previously been a Carter slave. Winifred L. Carter (later Brooke) sold land and, I believe, slaves to John B. Kerfoot. There probably is a deed in Fauquier County to confirm this. Caroline's children are listed (with ages) in Fauquier County chancery case 1843-002. The ages are likely taken off the deed that I haven't pulled yet. Caroline's children are Eliza, Emoline, James, Henry, Alfred, and Melvina. Kerfoot was also in debt and the court case was an effort to force the sale of land and slaves. Alonzo is the son of William Massey. As noted above, William was not sold to Blackwell. I think he may have been sold and moved to South Carolina. Alonzo Massey enlisted with the South Carolina infantry colored troops during the civil war. There is also a William Massey who enlisted with a South Carolina artillery troop, though the age isn't given so I can't prove if this is the same William Massey.

The colored troop civil war records are available on Ancestry. Alonzo's widow, Jenny (she remarried after Alonzo's death to someone named Ambrose) filed for a pension, which led me to Alonzo's records. Alonzo's marriage record to Jenny Cook shows that his parents were William and

Polly (aka Mary) Massey. James Massey, one of the sons of Caroline and Edward, also served in the civil war colored troops. He enlisted in New Orleans, LA. His civil war records show that he was born in Fauquier County, VA. Edward Massey (the younger who married Margaret Taylor) was also a son of Edward and Caroline Massey, i.e. a brother of Melvina. He was not included in the list of Caroline's children in the court case because he was not born yet. His marriage record provided his parent's names. That is probably the best of what I found. There are a smattering of death certificates for children that were helpful. They are attached to my Cook Family Tree. Oh, and no, I am not related to the Cook family either. I just enjoy researching family history. Which reminds me...do you have any dna matches to the Carter family?

I was wondering if you are related to this guy who is an ancestor of Moore F Carter:

www.novahistory.org/FryingPan/FryingPanCopperMine.htm

Debbie

September 12, 2016

"Judith Carter's son-in-law, James Blackwell, purchased Mima and her children Jane, Edward, John, and Lucian. He also purchased Morton, but the court case does not say if he is related.

Blackwell allowed Judith to retain physical possession of all of the slaves he purchased. If you look at the 1850 slave schedule for Judith Carter and James Blackwell, you will find a lot of their slaves identified as mulatto. If you want to share my name, that is fine.

It is nice to be part of the adventure. You probably figured out my name is Debbie Robison. Doh is from the Simpsons. :-) I first started looking at Judith Carter's records when I was searching the Fauquier County birth register for a mother named Grace giving birth to a daughter named Alice (Grace Massey is in the 1870 census with

Alice).

Judith Carter was listed as the owner so I thought I'd see if I could find other members of Grace's family listed in the chancery cases for confirmation. The birth register is the only potential paper trail to the Carters so far.

The rest just works out because the names and approximate ages generally match. The sad thing about the Fauquier County birth register is that for years after 1853 the registrar no longer included the names of the slave births so I cannot check to see if the Grace that was owned by Judith Carter had other children that match Grace Massey's children. I put in an order through interlibrary loan for the Fauquier County death register. I'm hoping this will have some names I need for confirmation. It takes a couple weeks for the microfilm to come in. Judith's husband, Moore Fauntleroy Carter, was the half-brother of 'Gentleman Jim' Robinson. Moore and Jim share a father: Landon Carter II. Jim is mulatto. You can google him. *

*It will be interesting to see if a Carter male is the progenitor, and who that might be. That is an interesting idea about Jemima. I'll need to be on the lookout for that name too."

September 13, 2016

"I'm feeling better about the Carter connection every day. Still not a slam-dunk, but I think this is a solid lead. I just noticed that James and Grace Massey were living next door to Helen Edmonds in 1870. Helen was the daughter of Moore F and Judith Carter.

This is significant because James and Grace Massey list a daughter named Blanche in the 1880 census. (recall Blanche Macy is living with her sister Margaret Ruffin in 1900). And Margaret Ruffin is reportedly the niece of Melvina Massey."

September 14, 2016

"The plot thickens. In 1824, William Massey was paid $6.75 by Judith Carter administrator of the estate of Moore F. Carter. This info is from the estate accounts filed in the will books.

In the 1810 census, there is a white overseer in Fauquier co named William Massey. In 1780, Maj. Thomas Marshall sold 1,000 acres to Maj. Thomas Massey, part of his Oak Hill estate near Delaplane (so near the Carters). This places a wealthy white Massey family in very close proximity to Mima. I need to do a family tree for this white Massey family to see what turns up.

Also, there is a day book that was written by Moore F Carter in the Va Historical Society archives that covers the first few years of the 19th century. That may have some answers."

September 23, 2016

"I checked a voter list for West End in the township of Falls Church for an election held on 5 Nov 1872 and found that William Massey voted. He was identified on the rolls as colored. I did not see any other Massey family members who voted at that precinct.

Someday I'll check the other precincts. (Requires going to the courthouse during work hours.) This is quite an interesting find, though, because now we have proof that a William Massey lived in the area. I think he is the father of Alonzo Massey."

September 26, 2016

"In 1871 when the land was sold to the Trustees of the Second Baptist Church of Falls Church, the trustees were Eli Blackwell, Andrew Tillman, and James Lee (as noted in the deed)."

November 20, 2016

"After I noticed that the Masseys lived next door to the Carters, I wondered if any of your dna matches have Massey in their tree. What do you make of the research into a Fauquier County line? Do you know of any male cousins who descend directly down through the male line so that yDNA could be compared to the Massey Family DNA project?

December 13, 2016

"I just found where George Cuthbert Powell, who owned a 13 year old slave named Melvina in 1849 (I think this is your Melvina) was first cousins with Ellen D Powell. She married William H Gray, Joseph Glass Gray's brother so William H Gray might be a person of interest to research." Debbie

Negro Burned to Death.

FARGO, N. D., March 24.—Fire at 1 o'clock a. m. destroyed the frame building in the First ward owned and occupied by Melvina Massey as a sporting house. The only occupants were two colored men named William Davis and John Griffith, both of whom had come from Moorhead a short time before, and were very drunk. Davis was burned to death.

Crystal Palace burns down, and is rebuilt a year later. - National Archives

Sentenced Melvina to 1 year confinement. She was only the second person ever prosecuted for bootlegging.

The supreme court has for the second time sustained a conviction and penitentiary sentence for violation of the prohibition law, where the case was brought under that portion of the prohibition law which empowers a judge of the district court, without a jury, to sentence to the penitentiary for a second offense. This is in the case of ██████ ██████ the colored keeper of a resort at Fargo, who was sentenced to a year in the penitentiary for violation of an injunctional order issued by Judge Pollock. The other case was that of Norman Markuson of Valley City, who was sentenced to a year by Judge Glaspell. In that case the question of the power of sentence to the penitentiary for contempt without a jury was brought up, and finally went to the supreme court of the United States. Markuson had to serve his term from which he was recently released.

Melvina loses her appeal. National Archives

Times are high in Fargo. Late Saturday night all of the gambling houses were raided and closed by the police. Madame Massey's house was also pulled and seven men and three inmates, all colored, jailed. 'Tis said there will be no more gambling in Fargo under the present administration.

Melvina raided for gambling. National Archives

Bismarck Penitentiary

Warden's Quarters and Admin Building

This is where Melvina is reported to have served her time, and not in the women's cell within the main confinement area. Building was moved in 2012. # Jealousy

A CASE OF JEALOUSY.

Malvina Massey, charged with threats to Lewis Davis, husband of Henrietta Davis, proves to be a first-class case of jealousy. The testimony developed the fact that Lewis, a rather dandy colored man, made the acquaintance of Malvina Davis, tall, with lustrous eyes, with whom he became intimate in Chicago, she promising to become his wife. He came to Washington and seeing Henrietta, a bright and rather good-looking mulatto, was smitten with, wooed, and married her. Malvina followed her truant lover, and finding she could not retain the affections of Lewis, has frequently threatened both him and his new wife, to whom he was married last Wednesday night. Lewis produced some letters which Malvina had written to him, in which threats were made to go for him in case he married Henrietta. Malvina, in the dock, eyed Lewis closely while he gave testimony, when she told the court that instead of making positive threats she only said what ought to be done to Lewis for doing her so dirty a trick as he had done her. The court saw how it was, and took Malvina's personal bond to keep the peace on Mr. and Mrs. Lewis Davis.

This case leads to the 'Breach of Promise' trial.The Journalist mixes up the names. National Archives

BREACH-OF-PROMISE SUIT.

Melvina Massey has sued Lewis P. H. Davis in the Supreme Court of the District of Columbia, claiming $5,000 for breach of promise of marriage. She claims that he promised her marriage, but although she has always been ready to marry him, he has refused, on demand, to marry her, and has married another.

No actual settlement. Melvina goes back to Chicago. National Archives

Note is No Good.

Anyone who buys a promissory note given by a woman of the restricted district is running the risk of losing all he paid for it. If he tries to collect in the courts he runs a risk of losing quite a bit more. These conclusions are suggested by a verdict returned yesterday afternoon in the district court at Fargo by which Attorney Taylor Crum was denied a judgment of $100 against Melvina Massey, a notorious negro denizen of the old red light district.

When the crusade against the "hollow" was on last fall the Massey woman retained a Bemidji lawyer of her own race. When his labors ended she gave him a note for $100 in payment for his services. This note he sold to Attorney Crum, who, when he tried to collect on it, had to go to court. The case was taken to Judge H. F. Miller's court, and Crum lost. It was appealed to the district court and yesterday Crum lost again. The note, the jury believed, was given in payment for services of an illegal nature, and therefore was null and void.

Library of Congress National Archives

assignation made complaint to him yesterday that Bell attempted to persuade
them to give him collateral sufficient
in an amount to guarantee protection.
They did not fall in with his brilliant,
but not visionary scheme, for they do
say whatever Bell is, he is not visionary.
It is alleged that the amateur detective
called upon Madame Massey and said
he had a great mind to close all the
other disreputable houses and leave her
place open provided she would make the
trouble worth the while.' It is alleged
that Bell said $100 would be needed to
bring about such a state of things. The
madame turned pale, she said, and then
notified the police. It is also said that
Bell approached a woman call Peart
and made her the same proposition only
the figure was a trifle lower. It is
charged that he asked only $20
but this he did not get. Chief Barnes
is busy investigating the charges.

He tried to strong arm her- National Archives

The Church, The Brothel, and water

And This in Fargo.

Fargo Forum: Religion and sin have their water pipes mixed in the First Ward. The Norwegian Baptist church is erecting a new edifice and needed water connections for the baptismal font. It was first proposed to connect with the water pipe to Rusch & Smith's slaughter house but that cost too much. so connections were finally made with the water pipe at Madame Massey' house of ill fame for $10.

Church uses Melvina's water to fill their Baptimal pool. National Archives

1902 Trial

The charge against ~~Madame Massey~~ for selling liquor at Fargo was dismissed when the case came to hearing. The prosecuting witness forgot his lines.

He forgot his lines - National Archives

About the Author

Author, Screenwriter, James Lee Nathan III

James Lee Nathan III (JLN3), is the self-published author of two novels and nine novellas, spanning many speculative fiction sub-genres. JLN3 is best known for his scifi erotic crime drama series Robert Manis and No Brakes, both of which are bestsellers on the leanpub author platform.

His latest works, CRIME-PHYTER, and Ibrahim Unites

introduce readers to his Next Level Fiction experience. James is from East Elmhurst, Queens, NY.